THE DEFENDER

#12

NO
SURVIVORS

Books by Jerry Ahern

The Survivalist Series

The Defender Series

They Call Me the Mercenary Series

THE DEFENDER

#12

NO
SURVIVORS

JERRY AHERN

SPEAKING VOLUMES, LLC

NAPLES, FLORIDA

2013

THE DEFENDER

#12 NO SURVIVORS

ISBN 978-1-61232-319-0

For all the readers who've followed the adventures of David and Rosie and all the Patriots, many thanks; keep the faith. . .

CHAPTER ONE

*T*he January wind blew stiff and cold out of the north. The fabric that was draped liberally over the statue billowed with the wind's force. Almost tantalizingly, for a split second it would outline what lay beneath in startling detail. Then the wind shifted again and all true shape vanished.

"These years are now behind us," he went on, "but the memory of these years will never die, even when all those of us who survived them have eventually perished. The United States, in 1776, was the greatest of human experiments. But because some forgot why this country was born and what had made this country great, the nation very nearly succumbed.

"As I campaigned for this office, I told the American people what I intended to accomplish in my administration. Some told me that what I spoke of was political suicide. But I learned in those years, from my mother and my stepfather and from those they fought beside, that enough lies had been told already, that the reason why our country was in a state of chaos and violence was, indeed, because of the lies.

"I pledged to work for fewer laws, less government intrusion, a return to freedom, the supremacy of the individual. And I renew this commitment now. Government's purpose is to serve those individuals from whom government receives its authority; it has no other purpose. To achieve those ends, as I promised in my campaign and intend to live up to in my administration, I will bend every possible effort to ensure that no elected official in the United States is able to succeed himself in office." The multitudes assembled before the Capitol Building applauded, shouted. "I seek to guarantee this by a constitutional amendment." Applause thundered again. "And I mean every office, from city councilman to board of education member to mayor to governor to senator to congressman to President." People stood, applauding, shouting, and he waited until they quieted because even over the public address system he knew he would not be heard. "I will remain in office only long enough to see this goal accomplished. If it is accomplished in these four years to which I have been elected, at the end of these four years I shall not stand for reelection. If the achievement of this goal takes beyond four years, as soon as this goal has been achieved I will step down." There were shouts of "No" ringing from all sides, from all around him.

He looked at the covering over the statue, turned, and looked behind him at his mother, at his stepfather, at his wife, who sat there on the platform. There was the same quiet dignity in his stepfather's eyes that was always there, the dignity of strength; there were tears in the eyes of his wife and the eyes of his mother.

He looked back toward the crowd that covered the Hill and overflowed onto the Mall area. "We would not be here today were it not for a group of men and women known as the Patriots."

The audience became silent, hushed.

His throat tightened as he looked toward the still covered statue. "Without—without their efforts, today there would be no United States of America."

He closed his eyes for a moment, unable to go on, the silence palpable now. David Holden. Rosie Shepherd. Tears welled up in his eyes.

CHAPTER TWO

Clark Pietrowski—he still looked a little pale, but insisted he was fully recovered—told her, "This is a great idea, if it doesn't get you killed, Rosie." He opened the cylinder on his double-action Smith & Wesson revolver.

"I was looking for an excuse to wear this anyway," Rose Shepherd told him, touching at her skirt. She smiled, then leaned over and kissed him on the cheek. "You old fart, you worry too much. And if I get killed, you'll probably get killed too." Then she started to slip her arms into her coat, Clark, setting the gun on the drive shaft hump, helping her. She reached under the long, open sweater she wore, touching at the revolver holstered beneath her blouse. "I tell you, Clark, when this is over, if we live through it, you know what I'm looking forward to?"

"No, kid, what?" Clark smiled, closing the .357's cylinder and making the handgun disappear under his coat.

"Remember in the sixties, when women were burning their bras?"

"Yeah. That's not all they burned." And he laughed a little.

"No, I'm serious. Well, I'm gonna burn my BDUs. I'm tired of dressing like a guy most of the time. You know how good it feels to wear nylons and a slip and—"

Clark Pietrowski laughed. "Honest answer? No, I don't know. But I'll take your word for it, Rosie."

Rose Shepherd shook her head, laughed a little, thought of the old days before the Patriots took up the fight against the Front for the Liberation of North America, when she was just a plainclothes cop. Sometimes, she couldn't wait to get home, get out of her clothes—a skirt and blouse or dress, pantyhose, heels, the whole works—and get into blue jeans or sweats. Maybe part of it was David, that loving him made her feel more like a woman than she had ever felt before knowing him.

And that feeling with him was the most important thing that had ever been in her life or ever would be.

"Be careful," Clark told her as she started out of the car.

"Right." She nodded. What did he think she'd do, be reckless?

She snugged her coat around her against the night's cold, her bag slung from her left shoulder, the flap open so she could get at the blackened Detonics Servicemaster just inside.

The skirt she wore—a muted, blue-black plaid—was wool and lined and came to the middle of her calves. With her boots—not combat boots, but the kind with high heels—and her coat, which was about the same length as the skirt, she was amply warm except for her hands. There were lined leather gloves in her coat pocket, but she wouldn't be as adept at manipulating a gun if she wore them, so she left them where they were.

She walked along the damp slicked tarmac driveway toward the high chain-link fence, her eyes on the gates. They were locked, just like they were the first time she'd seen them, locked with a padlock and a length of chain wound several times around the gates' verticals. Beyond the fence was the nondescript, flat-roofed concrete building she knew was just a shell, a facade to disguise what lay beneath.

She approached the gates, wondering if anyone was

watching. She'd had people from the Metro Patriot Cell watching the onetime Delta Force facility for two days and nights nonstop. There had been no sign of any activity whatsoever, no one entering, leaving, no guard movements, no lights, nothing.

In her pocket was a duplicate of the key Luther Steel had used that very first time she and David had come here, used to open the padlock on the gates. That the lock had never been changed was too much to hope for. There were heavy-duty cutters hidden in the trunk of the Ford, and her people, surrounding them at varying distances from the facility and masked by the darkness, had explosives. Getting past just a lock wouldn't be a problem, but what if the Presidential Strike Force were waiting for her inside?

She quickened her pace slightly, not stopping until she stood just beside the gates. She reached into her coat pocket for her gloves, pulled them out, casually flicked them against the fence to see if it were electrified before she touched it. It was not.

Clutching her gloves in her left hand, with her right hand she shook on the fence. She called out, "Hello? Inside? Is there anybody there? My father and I are lost. Hello?"

Then Rose Shepherd waited, tapping the toe of her right boot impatiently against the driveway surface like the well-off Yuppie she was dressed as.

There was no answer, no lights went on. Nothing happened. She called back to Clark Pietrowski, just as planned. "Daddy! Honk the horn, please!"

After a second, Clark obliged, honking the horn three times, long blasts that only a deaf person would not have heard.

"Hello?" Rose Shepherd shouted again.

There was no answer.

She put her gloves in her pocket and reached into her

purse. Beside the .45 automatic was the key. She put it into the padlock and turned.

A little stiff from disuse, but the lock opened. . . .

Geoffrey Kearney sat alone on the rocks beside the surf. He cleaned his guns. The rocks were black, but not as black as his thoughts.

Linda Effingham's death was not just something that happened. She was murdered. And the reason why was clear. The surf roared in, withdrew timidly. They wanted him to be their fair-haired boy, the spokesman—clean-cut and apple-pie nice—for the Front for the Liberation of North America. And a girl who had a drinking problem didn't fit the image. Ricardo Montenegro, upon "learning" of Linda's demise, had said, "Remember the old saying, my friend, that women are like streetcars. But hey, you are too young to remember streetcars, Thad. But remember, they are like streetcars. Another one's always coming along."

Thad Borden nodded, pretended to understand, take comfort from the drug dealer's words; meanwhile, inside Thad Borden, Geoffrey Kearney barely restrained himself from murder.

It wasn't that he couldn't have killed Dimitri Borsoi, alias Mr. Johnson, and Ricardo Montenegro, drug-dealing money man for the FLNA. He could have, but Borsoi's collection of filthy-mouthed witless streetpunks would have closed in. And somewhere inside himself, Geoffrey Kearney knew that the one thing he must not do to honor Linda's memory was to give his own life; she would not have wanted that.

But if the sacrifice of his life proved the only means by which he could take their lives, he would do it regardless.

Yet he would have to wait. Because when he killed, he

wanted not only to kill Borsoi and the disgusting, pock-marked Montenegro, but to deal a fatal blow to the FLNA.

For that, he would need to bide his time.

He had the smaller of the two 9mm Smith & Wesson semiautomatics cleaned and reassembled; after loading it, he unloaded the larger pistol and began to fieldstrip it.

When it came, it would come violently, that opportunity that was his heart's desire; but it could come neither soon nor violently enough. . . .

Thomas Ashbrooke slept heavily when he was in bed with his wife, Diane, but never when he was in bed alone. Despite an offer from a beautiful girl young enough to be his daughter, an offer that many men his age would have found irresistible, he slept alone tonight.

And his eyes were fully open, fully accustomed to the dark. Both the SIG-Sauer P-226 and the smaller P-228 were ready to hand, the larger gun in the Galco Miami Classic shoulder rig hung under his jacket on a chair near the bed, the smaller gun out of the ankle holster and under the second, unused pillow beside him.

Slowly, Thomas Ashbrooke moved his left hand upward toward that second pillow. His fingers slipped beneath it, closed around the butt of the 228, his right first finger going into the trigger guard, resting against the trigger as his hand drifted downward and under the sheet that covered him.

In the hot countries, there was always risk, more so than elsewhere, it seemed, assassins and their ilk attracted to the desperation of warmer climates; or at least that was his experience. He had told himself, he would be safe here in Israel, that remaining armed was only perfunctory, the Mossad on his side, his ally. He was reminded of the biblical quotation, "I will say of the Lord, He is my refuge and my fortress: my God; in him will I trust."

Someone stood against him on the patio outside the French doors leading between it and his bedroom. He'd seen a flicker of movement when he rolled over and opened his eyes. He assumed some telltale sound had aroused him. But still, he would have dismissed that. Then there was a sound he could not dismiss. One of the flagstones in the patio floor was loose; Ashbrooke had almost tripped over it himself less than a day ago. Whoever stalked him had done the same.

The SIG rested in his left hand, but across his abdomen now, pointed toward the French doors.

He breathed easily, but could feel sweat starting under his armpits.

A glance at the bedside clock showed almost four A.M. So it was hardly the maid coming to pick up or a gardener.

He tried formulating a plan and listening at the same time. If one assassin alone had been sent against him, alerted he stood a very good chance, better than the assassin did, really. But such things were often carried out by teams of men in this part of the world, where life could be bought awfully cheaply, life and death.

There was merit to the idea of a team because a single assassin would have been good enough not to make betraying sounds, maybe even avoid the noise of that loose flagstone.

Two, perhaps three, four unlikely (the fourth man, if there were one, would be keeping the getaway car ready for instant flight). Thomas Ashbrooke began surveying the room, trying to ascertain the most likely entry points and, therefore, required fields of fire. He had, of course, analyzed the bedroom in such a manner before he'd closed his eyes on the first night of his return here to Israel after the arms delivery to the Patriots. But review was in order, and there seemed a few seconds for it.

Someone would come from the patio, perhaps two someones. And the other likely approach would be right in through the bedroom door.

He decided now. Three men. That would account for no alarm being raised by the Mossad man guarding the house. Officially, the fellow didn't exist, but Ashbrooke had noted the car and, through a friend who was unofficial but had the right contacts, had confirmed that the car parked so unobtrusively was, indeed, Mossad.

Three men, the chap sent by the Mossad dead, which either meant a very good suppressor-fitted gun, a crossbow, or a knife. In this part of the world, the latter was the most probable, the Mossad the ones with the good silencers and not that terribly many persons adept with a crossbow, despite their excellent utility.

Ashbrooke exhaled.

Logic dictated—what did logic dictate? The bedroom door man would be waiting outside for him, in case the two on the patio caused an alarm of any sort that spooked the game or just plain missed in their try.

Ashbrooke eyed the door.

A trap, but could he turn it to his advantage?

He thought so, certainly hoped so.

It was time to get out of bed and find out.

Tom Ashbrooke kicked the covers away, swung his right foot to the floor and—naked—all but ran across the room, the chair overturning as he grasped for the shoulder holster beneath his coat, catching it, letting it slide down his right forearm to his elbow as he flattened himself along the wall. He was sometimes amazed that his body, after more than sixty years of hard use, could respond as fast as it did when he needed it to. But this was a younger man's game and he knew it.

He moved along the wall, slipping the Galco rig's harness over his shoulders, his right hand grasping the butt of the full-sized SIG-Sauer P-226, popping the thumb break and freeing the 9mm from the leather.

A pistol in each hand now, Ashbrooke moved along the wall as rapidly as he could in silence, crossing around an overstuffed chair, past the bathroom door. It was open, and no one was inside the bathroom. He snatched a towel off the rack, set down his pistols on the arm of the chair, wrapped the towel around his waist, picked up both pistols again, and continued on toward the bedroom door. But he kept his eyes constantly on the French doors leading to the patio.

Beside the bedroom door now—the door was partially ajar, just as he'd left it—Ashbrooke stopped, dropping down behind a dresser of diminutive proportions, but seemingly built of sturdy materials. He was three feet or so from the chair.

It wasn't a brilliant plan he'd formulated, but it was the best one he could muster. Ashbrooke fired the larger pistol into the mattress, a double tap, then another and another. He stepped back quickly. With his bare right foot, he kicked the overstuffed chair away from the wall and onto its side with a loud thud, then made a sound halfway between that of a constipated man groaning and a cough as he took cover again behind the dresser.

He waited, the larger SIG trained on the patio doors. As soon as someone stepped into view and he had a clean target, he'd fire, smash out the glass, and hopefully nail whoever was trying to get him. The smaller SIG he held on the bedroom door, his attention all but riveted there.

And he heard movement.

Coughing, he groaned, "Help me!"

There was still no movement from the patio, and this was starting to worry him.

From the other side of the bedroom door, he heard a

voice, the sound gravelly, low, just above a whisper. "Achmed?"

Ashbrooke couldn't help it; he smiled.

"Achmed?"

Ashbrooke coughed again, drawing back into the protection of the dresser.

The man belonging to the voice was just at the door now because the door swung back, kicked, and two shots were fired into the ceiling. Ashbrooke aimed the 228 at about belt level and fired through the wall, zigzagging the muzzle up and down and right and left, emptying the pistol, then dropping the slide stop to let the slide run forward over the empty magazine. He pulled the 228's double-action trigger several times, the clicking sound loud. He swore under his breath, but loudly enough that he hoped his assailants would hear.

The glass in the French doors shattered as a flagstone punched through it.

Ashbrooke held his fire with the larger pistol, the 226. Ten rounds were still in the gun. His eyes moving back and forth from the patio to the bedroom door, he set the smaller 228 beside his left knee, buttoned the magazine release, then drew a fifteen-round spare for the 226 from the Galco holster's offside pouch. He slipped the magazine up the well, then slowly, a little awkwardly as he still held the 226, worked the slide of the 228 as soundlessly as he could, chambering the top round. Now he had twenty-five rounds ready, both pistols cocked.

A man stepped out from the jamb on the left side of the French doors.

Ashbrooke mentally noted the weapon. An Uzi submachine gun, common enough here. The man started to open fire into the room, a second man emerging from the opposite side of the French doors, a riot shotgun in his hands.

As the submachine gun sprayed across the room, Ashbrooke rested his right elbow over his right knee, got a low point-shoulder position over the sights of the 226, and fired single action.

His bullet split into the upper bridge of the submachine gunner's nose, closer to the right eye than the left, the man's body sprawling back, the submachine gun firing out in a ragged arc along the bedroom ceiling and through the frame for the shattered French doors.

The man with the riot shotgun—he was dressed in dirty khakis and had a week's growth of beard—wheeled toward the origin of the pistol shot.

Ashbrooke fired both pistols simultaneously from chest level, a double tap from each, then another double-double tap, the riot shotgun discharging into the dresser beside Ashbrooke as the man sprawled back dead.

Ashbrooke was up, moving, changing to a new position of cover behind the chair.

With the chair at an angle, the greatest part of its bulk was between him and the opening for the bedroom door, and he had at least marginally adequate cover from the wall in case anyone still lived in the hallway beyond the bedroom door and tried Ashbrooke's own trick against him.

Ashbrooke counted off the seconds.

A full minute.

Two.

Emergency vehicle sirens in the distance.

Ashbrooke got up to a crouch, made a quick dash for the bedroom door, kicked it closed, the door bouncing back toward him.

He fired two shots high, crossed to the other side of the

door as he made the door bounce again, flattened himself along the opposite wall.

Nothing.

A cocked pistol in each hand, Ashbrooke went through the doorway.

Sprawled on the floor was a man in ragged trousers and stained T-shirt, some of the stains blood. Blood and plaster dust were splattered all over his body.

Ashbrooke kept close to the wall as he stepped back into the bedroom.

He let out a long breath.

With three dead and emergency vehicles on the way, all he had to do was sit tight, wait, explain to whoever showed up by getting them to call his Mossad contacts.

But the shooting was over. He was alive.

The FLNA and the drug cartel run by rogue KGB personnel who financed it were out of luck this time.

It was a foregone conclusion they'd try again, but that went with the territory, Ashbrooke told himself.

He decocked both SIGs and waited there for the police.

CHAPTER THREE

*T*he G-3 slung cross body and under her right shoulder, clutched in both hands, Rose Shepherd felt a little foolish walking along through the corridors of the underground Delta facility.

It was absolutely empty, but she was determined not to let down the collective guard just in case.

But it was stupid, carrying an assault rifle while wearing a skirt and high-heeled boots.

Tom LeFleur and Randy Blumenthal, along with a half-dozen Patriots, came running back out of a side corridor, Rose Shepherd swinging the muzzle of the German assault rifle toward them, letting out a long breath. She wanted to tell Tom and Randy to shout or something. Instead of embarrassing them, she called out, "Anything?"

"Clean as a whistle," LeFleur shouted back.

"Nobody's down here or has been down here for it looks like a long time, Rosie," Blumenthal told her, sounding a little out of breath. He was little more than a kid, and sometimes she forgot that. "We're clear."

"Hold this corridor, and I'll be back." She started off toward the weapons room; Clark Pietrowski with a small force of Patriots was already there. As she found it and entered, she was amazed at her good fortune. The armory was just as she remembered it, smaller than the soundstage-like area that was the control center for the underground facility, but its walls lined with racks running back to back and facing each other across the center of the room. The east and west walls were piled high with crates of ammunition, while the north and south walls—narrower—were fitted with bins of spare magazines and related accessories, each bin clearly stencil-labeled. M-16s, 7.62mm Heckler & Koch G-3s, G-41s, HK-13 light machine guns, FIE/Franchi SPAS-12, LAW-12 and SAS-12 shotguns, MP5-SD3 H & K integral suppressor 9mm submachine guns, Beretta 92F (M-9) military pistols, SIG-Sauer P-226 pistols and Glock-17s, assorted suppressor-fitted pistols, gas, sound and light, concussion, and fragmentation grenades as well as LAW rockets and various miscellaneous equipment were in abundance.

"I feel like a kid locked up overnight in a candy store," Rose said without even thinking.

"Should I get 'em to pull up the trucks?"

She looked at Clark and nodded. "Yeah, but keep everybody on their toes. I expected trouble, and it's fine we didn't get it. But we still could." She let her G-3 fall back on its sling and took one of the weapons off the rack, the locks already opened. She checked for a firing pin. Present. She took one of the Beretta pistols, confirmed that it was empty and disassembled it, checked it for being functional. The guns weren't tricked up, were ready to be cleaned, loaded, and fired.

She called over her shoulder to Clark Pietrowski, "I want every spare magazine, cleaning kit, parts kit, everything, and all the ammo. Get some people on these LAW rockets fast. They can use them to cover our act here just in case the PSF shows up."

"Once we've got this stuff disseminated to Patriot cells in this area, let 'em show up," Clark observed.

Rosie nodded, said, "Amen to that, buddy."

She lit a cigarette and smiled, exhaling as she looked over the racks and racks of firearms. There was nothing a woman enjoyed more than a productive shopping trip.

CHAPTER FOUR

Smith took Lilly Twobears into his arms.

"Matthew—"

"It is all right, Lilly. Wisdom's more a man at his age than some men ever get to be. Not to bring him would be worse."

"I know that, but I've never had to face the prospect of losing both of you at once."

"More enlightened self-interest?"

"Yes." She laughed.

Smith kissed her hard on the mouth, the fingers of her right hand softly touching at his neck, her other hand pressed against his chest, but not pushing him away.

As Smith stepped back, Lilly whispered, "I love you."

Smith told her, "I know." And then he looked over his shoulder, saying, "Wisdom, we're mounting up." And Smith walked toward the corner of the cabin where both animals waited.

His right hand gripped the horn of the saddle, and Smith swung up onto Araby's back, her chestnut body quivering under him, ready to move. As he looked toward the cabin, Wisdom held Lilly in his arms briefly, kissed her cheek, then started toward his horse. "All right, baby," and Smith touched at Araby softly with the heels of his boots as he pulled gently right on her reins.

Araby reared slightly, wheeled right, and vaulted off

across the snow, Smith glancing over his shoulder. Wisdom, on the big gray with the black stockings, mane, and tail, was coming up fast. Smith drew back on Araby's reins, letting the boy get up alongside him.

Because there were PSF personnel everywhere in these mountains, Smith had emptied his own saddle scabbard of the Heckler & Koch rifle and passed it to Wisdom. The boy was a natural shooter, perfect hand-eye coordination, patience, and a solid skeletal frame. The HK-91 was slung across Wisdom's back as they rode now.

In a way, the rifle was the perfect gun for Wisdom, a child of freedom, someone who would grow into the name he bore, whose decisions about what was good and what was bad and what he should possess or should not possess would not be made for him. The rifle, of course, was one of those that the government not many years before the troubles had begun had, in its infinite silliness, banned for importation.

Smith turned Araby up a snow-drifted draw and toward the rim of the valley into the lower peaks bordering Trapper Springs. In their saddlebags was their lunch, which Lilly had packed for them. The morning was just coming on dawn, and Lilly had stayed up half the night baking, for no other reason than her son liked chocolate cake.

Smith was rather fond of chocolate cake himself.

They reached the top of the draw; five miles through the snow ahead of them they would arrive at the rendezvous at Dutchman's Caverns. The Patriots had left for the rendezvous the night before, by horseback with Lilly's brother, Bob.

Smith liked Holden, the former college professor, liked the man's cut, the way he thought a lot and said a little. And his courage. It was easy to see why the FLNA and the PSF would want Holden dead or captured. Because David Holden was as serious a threat to their campaigns of terror and disinformation as could be found: He was an honest and courageous man who wanted nothing out of this except freedom.

The corrupt politicians, the peddlers of violence and greed and lies, all of them, in the deepest recesses of what passed for their souls, feared honesty and courage most of all.

Smith reined in Araby, young Wisdom pulling up beside him. The boy adjusted the sling of the rifle.

"Heavy?"

"Didn't you tell me once, Matthew, that the burdens most difficult to bear were sometimes those that were most worthwhile?"

"Perhaps I did, Wisdom." And Smith urged Araby ahead, the boy riding beside him along the ridge. . . .

"My stepfather once told me that the burdens most difficult to bear were sometimes those that were most worthwhile," he said. The crowd was silent. Again, his eyes flickered toward the statue. The wind blew harder, pressing the fabric of the covering tight against it, molding cloth to stone. And then the wind shifted slightly, and the impression was gone.

"As your President, I have one goal, albeit multifaceted. That goal is this: that this nation should once again be the world's shining light of freedom. And freedom can only be possessed by individuals. Rights are individual, not collective; and so too are responsibilities. Responsible men and women have the right and the obligation to control their own destinies. It is the spirit of collectivism that nearly destroyed this land.

"Responsibility for individual action is individual, not collective, whether it's the drunk driver who blames a fatal accident on the alcohol he of his own free will consumed or the careless person who misuses a product through his own failure to understand properly its utility and then attempts to sue the manufacturer.

"If one man or woman errs, it is the fault of that one man or woman, not the instrumentality utilized in commission of that error, however heinous, nor of those other persons who through their diligence are able to utilize a similar or identical instrumentality responsibly.

"There was a time in this land when the individual was exalted, was relied upon to be an individual. And then those who sought to mold this nation to their own inferior standards in order to satisfy personal greed, in order to vent impotent anger, in order to shore up faltering ego, began to preach the doctrine that individualism was selfishness and that selfishness was not an expression of one's true self, one's true virtue, but an evil, a negative force that was somehow a tool for the destruction of others. Such selfishness had to be outlawed, banned, controlled, regulated, circumscribed. And in moving toward this, freedom—because it is individual, not collective—was nearly choked off.

"The ultimate expression of this philosophy of negativism was revealed in the attempt by such persons to deprive individuals of the most basic human right, the right to continue living as one sees fit. To sustain that right, when it in no way conflicts with the rights of others, one has the moral, philosophical, and personal mandate to take whatever measures might be necessary.

"Guns and weapons of all kinds became the hated object because, by means of these tools that are the product of man's mind and ingenuity, it might be possible for the individual to resist the state, to maintain his or her freedom even when what is decreed as law is in violation of the principles agreed upon by which authority such a state governs.

"The individuality of freedom was viewed as dangerous and had to be stamped out.

"Government forgot or never learned the basic principle that governs transactions between rational men and women; that principle is noninitiation of force. Government forced its will upon the governed, illegally, then sought to make powerless the governed so there could be no hope for the governed to exercise their right to resist a corrupt state that imposed its will without benefit of agreed-upon law or morality."

Again, the men and women gathered there in the January cold stood and cheered. . . .

Roman Makowski stepped down from Air Force One. It amused him that every aircraft in which he flew was automatically designated Air Force One. It could have been a crop-dusting biplane, a military jet, or, as was the case now, a helicopter gunship.

His assistant, beside him, reminded him, "The commander of the base is named Lieutenant Colonel Hackler, Mr. President."

"Yeah, right," Makowski told him.

Troops of the Presidential Strike Force in their distinctive camouflage fatigues and their new berets stood at attention for his review.

An officer—must be the base commander, Makowski thought—approached.

Music played over a loudspeaker system. It was "Hail to the Chief."

Makowski eyed the headquarters building and started walking toward it, his assistant calling to him from the helicopter pad, "But Mr. President—"

"Too fuckin' cold," Makowski snapped over his shoulder.

The officer was running up to him now, saluted. "Mr. President."

"Harper, good to see you. An urgent call I have to make. My regrets to your men."

"But—"

Makowski kept walking, telling the tall man with two pistols on his belt, "I'm the President. I'm supposed to walk around in this fuckin' cold? You walk around in it."

The headquarters building was just ahead, and over its doorway there were heat lamps installed.

Roman Makowski quickened his pace, the officer with the two handguns beside him still. "Perhaps later, Mr. President?"

Makowski stopped under the heat lamps, turned, and looked at the man. "I came here to see what progress has been made in breaking these captured rebel officers. And to lure this damned Holden and his Patriot killers out into the open. Two reasons. Pneumonia isn't the third. If you ask me, you'd be a damn sight better off having your men build more walls around this friggin' icebox than parading around like a bunch of toy soldiers."

President Roman Makowski pushed past the officer, and the doors opened magically before him, a pretty little blonde in camouflage fatigues—some kind of a clerk, he guessed— opening the doors. "What's your name?"

"Anderson, sir. Corporal Louise Anderson."

"You can show me around the base later tonight. I'll need you available at a moment's notice."

"Yes, sir!" She saluted.

He nodded.

She could show him around his quarters from one side of the bed to the other.

He heard Harper or Hamer's voice behind him. "Mr. President!"

There was a threatening edge to the voice. Makowski stopped, turned around. "Where's Hobie Townes?"

"One of the rebel officers was on the verge of breaking. Mr. Townes felt he'd be of more service on the spot with Dr. Masterson and Dr. Liggett."

"Liggett?"

"The camp doctor, Mr. President."

"Right. I want this young woman to show me to my quarters. I want your best bourbon, and I want two hours in which I can rest from the journey. If this rebel officer is about to break, I can see him later. If he doesn't break, no point in it."

"Yes, Mr. President."

He read the name tag. "Hackler. You strike me as a good man. Play your cards right and you could go far."

Hackler's voice sounded enthused, but his eyes looked hard, angry. "Yes, Mr. President." And then Hackler looked at the blonde, telling her, "You're to accompany the President, Corporal, and assist him in any way possible, carrying out whatever tasks he assigns. Is that clear, Corporal?"

"Yes, sir," she answered, standing at attention. She had a cute little ass, Makowski noticed.

She turned and looked up at him.

"Let's see where my room is," Makowski told her.

"This way, Mr. President," she responded, gesturing along the corridor to his right.

Makowski started walking. Behind him, he heard the doors opening and closing. It would be Hacker or whatever his name was going out to give some lie to that collection of ex-cons standing outside in the cold like a bunch of morons. Makowski didn't care what the lie was, and he knew the Presidential Strike Force personnel didn't really care, either. A clean uniform beat prison gray, and a gun and a little power beat sucking up to the prison guards.

Loyalty was a wonderful thing.

CHAPTER FIVE

*D*avid Holden's feet were a little cold, so he started to walk again. He'd volunteered for a tour on guard at the mouth of Dutchman's Caverns, the young Native American from the Kalispell Patriot Cell who'd had the watch since four A.M. looking frozen half-stiff.

Holden moved along the ledge, then down into the deeper snow, not surprised to find it warmer here for his feet, despite the fact that the walking was slower, harder. Snow, drifted high by the biting, almost cyclonically moving winds, came to his thighs. Holden tightened the sling on his G-3 a little to make certain he kept the action clear of the snow. The G-3 was a rugged gun, but there was no sense subjecting it to more abuse than necessary.

He walked past the mouth of the main cave. It was deceptively small on the outside. After walking slightly stooped over for several yards, suddenly a vastly high vault had opened before him, at its greatest height well over fifty feet, stalactites hanging from the ceiling, frozen in time it seemed.

After all of this was over, if he and Rosie survived, he wanted to bring her back to this country. Its raw beauty was incredible, violent yet peaceful.

"Rosie," Holden said under his breath.

He missed her more than he'd thought possible. It wasn't that he loved his dead wife and children any less; he simply loved Rosie more than any living person. Sometimes, in the brutal honesty of loneliness, he realized he loved Rosie as much as he had ever loved.

His soul had died when Elizabeth and the children had been murdered in the FLNA attack that commencement day at the university, a day that seemed at once so long ago and yet so fresh in his consciousness it could not have been more than yesterday.

Rosie had breathed life into him again.

Sometimes, he told himself—as if he were some sort of salesman trying to convince a skeptical prospective customer—all about the things that he and Rosie would do after the war for freedom was resolved, won. He would take her to Switzerland, and she could see his father-in-law, Thomas Ashbrooke, again, meet Elizabeth's mother, Diane. Rosie and Diane would like each other, Holden surmised.

And there would have to be some frivolous times.

He'd never taken Rosie out to a fancy restaurant, or dancing, or to a movie, or for an ice cream cone, never done any of those things with her. And you had to do those things with someone you loved, wanted to marry.

But by then of course, with the war over and everything, they would be married, the very first thing. And they'd have one hell of a wedding reception. Rosie could plan the wedding, large or small, that didn't matter, Women loved planning things like that. He remembered Elizabeth, their wedding. But the reception would have to be a big one. All the Metro Patriots, the Patriots from other cells around the country with whom they had worked, Luther and his ex-FBI agents.

Holden was certain of that, that once the fighting was ended and done, Luther Steel, Bill Runningdeer, Pietrowski, LeFleur, and Blumenthal would all be vindicated in their roles of assisting the Patriots under authority of the real

President, the man whose office Roman Makowski had assumed after seeing to the real President's assassination.

Makowski.

Holden shivered, fought the wind for a second, tore off a glove, and lit a cigarette. He preferred bumming them from Rosie. It was a running joke with her. As he exhaled, pulled his glove on, Holden walked on. Rationally, he knew that smoking constricted blood vessels and actually would make him feel colder, but it felt warmer, even if it were only psychological. After all, a burning cigarette was on fire.

Makowski.

As Speaker of the House, Roman Makowski had embodied all that had been going wrong in America these last years. Higher taxes, more laws, fewer freedoms, regulations at every step along the road of life, evisceration of the Bill of Rights, the more the better and the more paperwork needed to serve his dubious ends, the more it cost, and the more taxes could be raised. And the entire process could begin again.

President. Makowski. President.

The words did not go together, no matter how they were arranged, no matter how often they were spoken. They did not fall naturally off the tongue. And when said, left a bitter aftertaste.

Holden heard the sound of the chopper, glanced right and left, ran for the rocks about a hundred yards to his right, lost his footing a little, caught himself, then ran on, diving behind the rocks into snow, the snow up to his armpits when he crouched.

His eyes focused on the helicopter.

Was it a reconnaissance craft?

Or did it carry Roman Makowski to the fort so obscenely named after him?

No. Because there would have been a fighter or gunship escort, probably both.

But if Bob Twobears' intelligence was right and Roman Makowski was coming here or had already arrived, the chance to take Makowski alive and use him as a bargaining chip to end the violence would be too good to ignore.

And that was the rub: Was it also too good to be true?

David Holden thought that, that it was a trap, had to be a trap.

But sometimes even a trap was too good to pass up. . . .

Smith held Araby's neck down as gently as he could, the mare's eyes wide, but not with fear of him, he knew. "Easy, baby," Smith whispered.

Smith glanced up at the helicopter—it was almost over the horizon—and then at Wisdom. The boy held his mount well.

As they'd crossed out of a narrow little gulch, the helicopter was just suddenly there, the wind playing tricks on the ears and masking the sound until it was nearly too late to take cover. Smith had rolled out of the saddle and bulldogged Araby down into the snow, shouting to Wisdom to do the same, the boy responding, but getting his mount down with a little bit more difficulty and less speed. It wasn't, Smith reminded himself, something one did every day.

They kept their mounts as still as possible, waiting out the aircraft, Smith telling the boy, "If I ask for that HK-91, Wisdom, I'll need it rather rapidly."

"Yes, Matthew."

But now the helicopter was gone from sight.

And Smith slowly helped Araby start to stand, then jumped back, merely holding to her reins and her mane, vaulting up into the saddle as she came fully erect.

Wisdom tried the same, but the gray bolted and Wisdom fell on his rear end. Smith laughed. Wisdom, still on his butt in the snow, looked up at Smith and stammered, "You're a white man and I'm an Indian. How come you're a better horseman?"

"Few abilities, however associative to one's ethnic heritage, are so innate that they don't demand to be fully learned, Wisdom."

The boy nodded.

Smith had the gray's reins, handed them to Wisdom once the boy had brushed the snow from the HK-91. Then Wisdom, with a look of determination etched on his face, grabbed the saddle horn with both hands and swung up. Wisdom rearranged the rifle on its sling, nodded that he was ready, and Smith eased his boot heels against Araby's flanks.

Soon they would be at the rendezvous.

Smith had worried over bringing Wisdom along for this, but a boy would never become a man if he weren't given the chance to. And Smith respected Wisdom far too much to deny him that. . . .

"Thousands left the United States, for Canada, for Latin America, some even returning to Europe. As Americans, we cannot bear ill will toward those who chose not to fight to restore our home. But there were others—by the thousands —who capitalized on the violence and misery and disorder for no other motive than profit. They chose to initiate force. Today, I am directing FBI Director-Designate Luther Steel to make every effort possible to cooperate with all other federal and local and state law enforcement agencies to bring these persons to justice.

"I speak, of course, of the drug dealers who financed the Front for the Liberation of North America, the street gang thugs who became soldiers in this terrorist movement aimed at destroying the very fiber of our nation, of those foreign nationals acting without sanction of government and totally without morality to destroy America through violence merely to create a new source of wealth from ill-gotten gains. Before coming here today, I had what I can only refer to as a very meaningful conversation with the Soviet ambassador. As I had anticipated, the United States will receive every kind of cooperation required to track down those officials of the Soviet Committee for State Security who, without the knowledge of their government, sponsored the terrorist and narcotics network of which the FLNA was a part.

"But the worst criminals of all were those who masqueraded under the guise of a legitimate military unit, calling themselves the Presidential Strike Force. These men and women, common criminals handpicked from the worst prisons, both civilian and military, across the length and breadth of the United States, became a secret police and secret army, dreaded in every dark corner of the land.

"By executive order this day I am directing that any surviving members of that force, when found, will serve out the balance of the original sentences that were lifted that they might be inducted into the PSF. I am further ordering that certain high-ranking officers within the PSF be brought before the Senate Select Committee on the Troubles, that they be questioned—without offer of immunity—" The crowd rose almost as one, applauding, cheering. As the noise subsided, he continued. "That without offer of immunity, these persons be rigorously questioned in order to establish the network by which the PSF was able to operate. Anyone who knowingly contributed to the Presidential Strike Force's campaign of terror—whether supplying information, as informants, collaborators, or in any other fashion—will be permanently expelled from the United States. If the Congress will not give me such authority, I will issue a Presidential Proclamation, have these persons expelled, and deal with the Congress myself."

Applause rang out again.

In the first row of seats, he saw Luther Steel's gray head, nodding, eyes smiling. . . .

Luther Steel walked toward the mouth of the cave. What was he doing here?

Fighting for freedom, of course, but he had thought he was doing that by joining the FBI. And now, because of Makowski and Hobart Townes, Makowski's hatchet man, he was an outlaw, and Rudolph Cerillia, director of the Federal Bureau of Investigation, was murdered.

When Mr. Cerillia had first told him of the plan, he hadn't quite known how to take it. An opportunity, yes, not just for service, but also for an important task that could mold history; but dangerous too. With a wife and children, that was always a consideration, something that couldn't be ignored.

Steel stood in the mouth of the cave, feeling the wind, staring out into the heavily falling snow.

Rocky Saddler was watching them, keeping them protected. At times, Steel would call a certain public telephone and Saddler would answer, and then there would be a few precious moments to talk with his wife, find something to laugh about with his children, then talk with Rocky— "How are they really doing? Are you sure you weren't followed? Are the kids taking it all right?"—and then a too hurried good-bye to his wife, not knowing if he'd ever speak to her again, see her, hold her.

It was the same for all of the men who had been part of his Metro Task Force, its sole intent to establish a liaison with the Metro Patriots through Director Cerillia for the

President in order to better prosecute the war with the FLNA and bring the violence to an end.

Runningdeer came up to stand beside him, Steel glancing over at him, Runningdeer with his Uzi slung from his shoulder. "Luther?"

"What, Bill?"

"I think I'm gonna die here."

Luther Steel looked at his friend, didn't know how to respond, looked away.

CHAPTER SIX

*D*imitri Borsoi lit a cigarette, shook his legs to clear a cramp, Kearney guessed, stood up, and walked toward the pool. "Thad, this business with your girl was most unfortunate. And you know I really feel for you very deeply."

"Thanks, Mr. Johnson."

Borsoi smiled, shrugged his broad shoulders. "Listen, words are easy, but I really mean what I say. The loss of a loved one can be devastating."

Kearney found himself agreeing with that.

The wind caught Borsoi's hair, billowed Borsoi's shirt sleeves. The sun shone bright, but it was still a little cool, and Kearney was grateful for the goatskin A-2 bomber jacket he wore. Borsoi started talking again. "We have a window of opportunity, Thad. I hadn't planned on getting you started so soon in your new role as spokesman for the FLNA, and when this came up, I told myself maybe I shouldn't even mention it, with your loss so fresh in everyone's mind."

"That's all right, Mr. Johnson. She woulda been proud of me doin' this."

Borsoi smiled, genuinely it seemed. And he looked hard at Kearney as he said, "You have an attitude that I personally find very refreshing, Thad. I think we made the right choice. You're the image we want to project to the American people." Kearney found it almost amusing that he was the one picked to be the all-American boy and he was British. "This window of opportunity to which I alluded, Thad. President Makowski offered a public forum for the FLNA's agenda, on national television. We're going to take him up on it. I'll have the times and everything very shortly. Your speech is already being written. I want you to all but memorize it, but you'll still be reading from a prompter. But I don't want you to look like you're reading."

"I get ya, Mr. Johnson."

"This will launch you into your future, Thad, an important future, with all the things men dream about."

"I do have dreams, Mr. Johnson." His dreams were filled with murder. . . .

Kearney was sitting beside Luther Steel in the first row there on the Hill, the seated and the standing-room crowd spread out along the Mall in vast numbers. Wavy white hair blowing in the wind, perfectly cut overcoat, hands in his pockets.

"Much thanks for our victory goes to this nation's historic ally, Great Britain. Beset by troubles of her own, she did not ignore the plight of a friend." He knew that Kearney's mission for British Intelligence had been out of perceived necessity rather than altruism, but that did not at all diminish it. His mother and stepfather had taught him to distrust altruism.

Lilly Twobears put down her book. The house was cleaned, the huge dinner she would need to serve that night was cooking, she was tired from staying up so late to bake and getting up so early to make breakfast for Matthew and Wisdom.

A cup of coffee would do the trick.

A little chilly in the cabin, despite the fire in the hearth (it was cute the way Matthew and Wisdom were so overprotective of her, had left her enough firewood for a week rather than just a day), she tugged her shawl closer up around her shoulders.

She went into the kitchen and started making coffee. There was a small picture of Wisdom and Matthew hung on the wall opposite the sink, there among the spoon racks, the various little things. She stared at the picture. Wisdom had asked her once, "Why do mothers do what they do?"

"I don't know what you mean, Wisdom."

"I mean, well, you're up early for us, work hard for us all day long. Isn't that altruism?"

"No. Not at all."

"But it's not for yourself."

"Ohh, you're not thinking like a parent, Wisdom. It's pure selfishness of the best kind. I enjoy doing for you and for Matthew because I love you both. I mean, sure, sometimes I'm tired and I'd just like to roll over in bed and sleep, but I enjoy caring for the two of you, and for this house and everything. I enjoy it more than I enjoy sleeping a little extra. Because I love you both. And doing things like getting up and making breakfast or whatever, well that's a way of saying that I love you guys. It makes me feel good to do it. Do you understand?"

"I think I do."

She wondered, for a time, if he had. But especially in recent months, she knew now that he did. The same reasoning was behind her comparatively enormous woodpile because they were both gone today, the same reason was behind Matthew giving Wisdom his rifle to carry.

She was always amused at the term when she'd find it in a book, about loving selflessly. Without self, there could be no love.

Persons who did not truly understand love thought that it was totally unselfish, when in reality love was the most totally selfish thing in the world, beautifully selfish.

The teapot with which she heated water for her instant coffee was whistling. Already, without thinking of it, she'd placed a moderately heaping teaspoon of coffee into the bottom of a mug. She poured the boiling water over it now.

Wisdom was almost a grown man, she told herself, and Matthew would die before letting anything happen to him. That was something people didn't really understand. Matthew would die to save Wisdom because Wisdom was so important to him, truly like a son.

She had taught Wisdom many things, and Matthew had taught him more, certainly in the ways of being a man. But both of them had always taught him one thing over all others, that one cannot value anything without valuing oneself.

That was why this Dr. Holden and Agent Steel and Bill Runningdeer, like herself and Wisdom, Native American, fought against the FLNA and the Presidential Strike Force. They valued individual freedom enough to die for it because to them to be free was an intrinsic value, not just something okay or convenient or nice but not necessary enough that one should give one's life.

Maybe that was why there was this need to fight now, because not enough people understood the true nature of humanity.

Lilly held the coffee mug in both hands, warming herself by it. She would return to her book for a while, then find something else to do to while away the time until Matthew and Wisdom returned, until she could go on living rather than only exist in emotional suspension. . . .

David Holden had been introduced to them as they had arrived, all by horseback because of the rugged terrain and heavy snow. That the snow fell again now and the wind had picked up only served to make the meeting safer, covering tracks.

There were representatives here of all the tribes in the area, lodges of the Sioux, Cheyenne, Arapaho, Indian tribes he'd never heard of in old movie westerns or books, more than a dozen men ranging in age from the late thirties through the early sixties; with each man came several others, the more advanced the age the seemingly larger the entourage.

But the odd thing was they all looked like cowboys instead of Indians, cowboy hats of all shapes and sizes, hatbands feathered or silver-conchoed or merely braided; boots, some worn, some shiny despite the snow; trophy buckles and blue jeans and snap-front shirts. The younger men had long hair, one of them with dark brown hair halfway down his back, worn loose like a woman might, others with hair braided. Holden supposed it was a sign of Indianness, of being who they were rather than trying to look like someone else.

And there was an assortment of weapons, from lever action rifles and exposed hammer shotguns to bolt action rifles with scopes, and almost everything in between.

And now, David Holden stood before them.

They sat on blankets set onto the cavern floor or stood leaning against the cavern walls, smoking cigarettes or pipes, one man chewing on a cigar.

Matthew Smith—what an oddly Socratic man he was—smoked a long, thin cigar, and beside him stood the boy Wisdom Twobears. Looking at Wisdom made Holden think of his own son, dead, losing his life trying to defend the lives of his mother and two sisters.

Holden cleared his throat, suddenly tight-feeling. "I've met all of you just briefly, I know, but this war we fight hasn't left us much time for the civilities, I suppose. A lot of you must wonder why I've asked Bob Twobears to call you all here. I mean, you know that I'm going to ask you to fight, but maybe you don't know exactly why and for what.

"The man who calls himself President of the United States," Holden went on, "ordered that officers of the armed forces, both men and women, suspected of remaining loyal to the Constitution of the United States be rounded up and brought here in cattle cars, to be held prisoner, tortured perhaps, brainwashed, swung over to the side of the Presidential Strike Force or killed.

"Now, admittedly, it would be hard not to find some irony in asking American Indians to come to the rescue of the United States Army and other U.S. armed forces personnel." There was some laughter, a few smiled. "And why should men who were dispossessed of their traditional homelands at gunpoint and forced onto reservations be willing to risk their lives for a Constitution that in many ways has ignored their existence for two centuries?

"The only reason, I guess," Holden told them, "is because of all Americans you are the most American. You've watched our few moments of glory over the centuries since the white man came here, watched our follies, too. Whether or not the partnership has been fair or equal or just, this is a land we share. And maybe this is a chance for you to assert that fact in a way that cannot be ignored. I don't know. But I do know that color or ethnic background or anything else doesn't really matter when one has to choose between what is right and what is wrong. To ignore the injustice of today would be just as wrong as when my ancestors ignored the injustice of yesterday. Good men, when faced with evil, cannot ignore the moral imperative to fight, whether with words and ideas or arms.

"And now," David Holden said, "is a time for arms. In a

very few days, my men and I will join with Bob Twobears' Patriots and Matthew Smith and whoever else is willing to help us. However many that is, or however few, we're attacking Fort Makowski in order to effect the escape of those military officers because we need them to get their old units into the fight on our side, and because men of conscience cannot stand by and ignore an atrocity without becoming a partner to it themselves. I will have weapons for you as needed," Holden told them, banking on Rosie having hit the Delta base and found the guns and ammunition and explosive ordnance still there. "But even if for some reason my promised weapons should not arrive, even if we have to use those old hunting rifles and knives and rocks and anything else we can find, we cannot ignore what must be done.

"I want to know who I can count on."

There was silence, as stony and cold as the walls of the cavern themselves. Holden wished he had a cigarette to hand, but didn't want to lose eye contact in order to light one.

One of the older chiefs stood up with some difficulty from the blanket on which he'd sat. He took off his battered gray felt cowboy hat. It was high crowned, like something out of a 1940s B western. He wore a high-riding tooled belt holster at his right hip, threaded onto his blue jeans, the gun in it a Colt Single Action Army or good replica, weathered-looking stag grips on it.

He smoked a pipe, but removed it from his mouth now as he began to speak. "It is strange to hear a white man speak to Indians of honor. Was it honor to push us and push us and push us some more while our women and children starved and our young men fell into the self-destruction of poverty and drink and despair? Yet you speak to us of honor. And you know that we must answer. Honor lives in us. I think it lives in you. I cannot speak for all of my brothers here, but I can speak for my people. My young men will fight, my young women will fight as well. Those who are too old to fight can help in other ways. I wish to see this evil place, Fort Makowski, destroyed. I wish to see the evil that spreads across the land crushed. For my people, not for yours. But we can work together."

David Holden breathed.

He figured it was safe to light the cigarette now.

CHAPTER SEVEN

*R*ose Shepherd set down the radio headset. She was alone in the communications tent, had asked to be.

She'd told herself to tell David when he called via the complex radio link they had to Montana, and maybe it was the static, that he sounded so far away, maybe that was why she hadn't told him.

She knew when it had happened.

Not that long ago really, when she'd caught a grazing wound from a stray bullet, she'd had a blood test. Dr. Wong, who had always helped the Patriots, ever since the beginning, had left Metro, come to work with the Patriots full time. He told her that—Congratulations!—she had joined the ranks of those lucky women who could not take the pill because of the effect it had on their blood pressure.

So it was a diaphragm and contraceptive foam (when there was time for that).

She supposed that was the problem.

She'd told David, of course, and he hadn't seemed alarmed, told her that if she—Rose Shepherd exhaled long and loud.

She supposed that the real reason she'd insisted on bringing the weapons shipment to Montana under her personal supervision was so she could see David face to face and tell him.

There were options, of course. But she remembered David

telling her about the statue somewhere in Italy of Garibaldi's wife, a pistol in one hand and a baby in the other, the baby suckling at her breast.

However awkward that might prove, it was a better option than destroying a life she so desperately wanted to bring into the world, because it would be half her, half him. Wouldn't that be a victory for Makowski and Townes and Borsoi and all of their enemies, that she would have to destroy a baby so she could continue to fight them? A person had the right to choose what she wanted to do—have a baby, paint herself blue, shave her head—but she decided that she wanted this baby the instant Dr. Wong told her.

She'd had girlfriends who water-skied a few weeks before giving birth. Fighting a war couldn't be more demanding on the body than something like that, could it?

She was terrified that David wouldn't want it. On one level, she knew he'd never say that, but what if she felt that?

Rose remembered the look on Dr. Wong's face. "Rosie, you've got a situation, here."

"A lot of women have trouble with their period, don't they, when they're—"

"You don't have trouble with your period. You wouldn't have come to me after just missing it once if you'd thought it was that, would you?"

"No."

"Rosie, you and David, right?"

"Of course—ohh, my God." She knew the night. They'd been so tired and he'd been gone for two days, and it seemed so natural just then, not in a couple of minutes after she put the damn thing into her.

She closed her eyes as Dr. Wong said, "You're a very healthy woman. You should give birth to a fine child, Rosie. I think David'll be happy."

"Ohh, yeah."

"He will. You're barely getting started. You don't need to worry about anything, just be happy."

She'd told Dr. Wong thanks, then left.

Nobody else knew.

But sharing sun showers with the other women in the camp, it wasn't the sort of thing she'd be able to hide for very long. And she was eating like a ravenous bear the last few days.

David would send her away, to "be safe." That galled her. She could fight as well as or better than any man in the camp, except for David. And she'd turned into a darned good strategist, or was it tactician? She could never remember the difference.

Anyway.

Rose Shepherd stared at the radio. "David, I'm pregnant. You're going to be a daddy." She closed her eyes, shook her head. Why weren't things ever that easy?

CHAPTER EIGHT

With David Holden and Luther Steel, Smith and Wisdom rode up into the high ground overlooking the canyon, on the other side of it, on a peninsula of rock, Fort Makowski.

Smith propped himself on his elbows as he lay on his belly in the snow, peering through his binoculars.

Luther Steel was on his immediate right. "The place looks impregnable."

"Umm," Smith grunted.

From his far right, Dr. Holden observed, "You were right about that train. Going right up and knocking on the front door is the only way to get in there, short of flying."

Smith handed his binoculars to Wisdom. "Thanks."

Smith nodded. He said to Holden and Steel, "I considered an airborne attack, with hang gliders possibly, but there are not enough people satisfactorily adept with them that it would have worked, not around here at any event. We don't have enough air power, just one helicopter from Bob Twobears' reservation and about a half-dozen single engine fixed wing aircraft we could borrow." Fort Makowski was a system of interconnected blockhouses, surrounding a multi-storied central structure, this all in turn surrounded by high concrete block walls topped with barbed wire that was almost certainly electrified and had alarm wires interlaced through it. The only way in was through steel outer gates, deflection barriers, and a long gauntlet on either side of the two-lane road that also served the railroad tracks, the gauntlet on either side obviously mined and swept by machine gun emplacements. "The railroad is the only way, and that's a heavy risk."

"Am I going?" Wisdom suddenly asked him.

Smith turned and looked at the boy, thumbed his Stetson back off his forehead. "Well, Wisdom, it is going to be dangerous, but I'm sure you'd rise to the occasion. The problem is one of appearance, really, Wisdom. You see, everybody who rides that train is going to have to wear the uniform of the Presidential Strike Force. You'd just look too young. And anyway, we're going to need some good people manning those antiaircraft emplacements along the route the train takes, to keep whatever's left of Fort Makowski's air power off our backs. I think your talents could best be utilized in that capacity. And I'm not saying this because I want to protect you; it will be extremely dangerous manning one of those antiaircraft emplacements. But if someone were to get a close look at your face and realize your age, that could sabotage the entire mission, Wisdom."

"All right. Then I'll help out in one of the antiaircraft emplacements." He returned the binoculars. Smith took them, nodded. "I'd better check on the horses." Smith nodded again.

As he looked away from Wisdom, he realized that Holden and Steel were looking at him. "Gentlemen?"

"My son would have been about his age," Holden said abruptly, then picked up his binoculars.

Smith said nothing. . . .

Rose Shepherd was stowing her gear in her pack, all of it very practical, black battle dress utilities, an extra pair of boots, extra black T-shirts, a heavy black woolen sweater.

She threw the sweater down on the top of the pack and dropped to her knees on the ground cloth and blanket bed.

She closed her eyes, but that didn't do any good.

The tears came anyway.

CHAPTER NINE

"**M**y name is Emma," she said.

"Hi, Emma."

"Can I come in?"

Geoffrey Kearney looked at her hard because he knew why she'd been sent. She wore a cotton-lined long wind-breaker that would have been large on him, blue jeans that fit her tight as a second skin, and an orange knit top that showed lots of cleavage and abdomen down to the navel. Past-shoulder-length blond hair, a very young, pretty face. "Come in."

She stepped into his bedroom and, with something akin to shyness, didn't close the door. "I was real sorry to hear about your girl."

"Thanks."

"You loved her a lot, I guess."

"Yeah." He was tired of doing American accents, tired of the whole charade. Kill Borsoi and Montenegro and be done with it. Not yet. "What can I do for ya?"

"Mr. Montenegro sent me by, to, uhh—"

He knew exactly why Montenegro had sent her by. "I'm really kinda tired, sweetheart."

She didn't start for the door. Instead, "Could I talk to ya?"

"Sure," Kearney told her.

She knitted her fingers together, her hands over her bare abdomen. "If, uhh, if—"

Kearney lit a cigarette in the blue yellow flame of his Zippo. "If what?" Dammit, he wasn't about to make it easier for her.

"If I don't, uhh—he'll—"

"What? Slap you around a bit?" Watch the accent, Kearney told himself.

Her eyes were pretty, pansy blue, frightened. She nodded her head, her eyes down as though she were studying the patch of carpet between them.

"You don't belong to anyone, do you? I mean, aren't you free to make up your own mind?"

"Could I have a cigarette?" He nodded, shook one free of the pack, even lit it for her, pocketing the cigarettes and the lighter again. "No filter. Do you break 'em off?"

"No. I buy them that way."

"I didn't know they made them that way."

"How old are you? Truth."

She cleared her throat. "Nineteen."

"God." And Kearney turned away from her, inhaled hard on his cigarette, so hard the tip glowed. "So, Montenegro sent you over to lighten my spirits." To hell with the accent for now.

"All he said was to go to bed with you, or whatever."

"Whatever?"

"You know," she said softly.

He was very angry. "No, I don't know. Tell me. What did he mean?"

"I—"

He turned around and looked at her. "What? Blow job? Or maybe I'd get my rocks off kicking the crap out of you?"

She looked away, actually sniffed.

"And if none of these delights interests me now?" Kearney asked her.

"He'll hit me."

"Has he hit you before?"

She nodded.

"Where?"

She turned her back to him, let the lined windbreaker fall from her shoulders. Then she did something with the little elasticized thing that barely covered her nipples in front. He could already see the beginnings of the marks, but when she pulled her top down, he could see them completely. A very skillful job with a belt, the sort of skillful job that only came through considerable practice.

"Montenegro did that?"

She only nodded, didn't turn around.

"He'll do it again if I don't have sex with you?"

She nodded again.

He wanted to tell her to sit down and finish her cigarette and lie a lot. But Montenegro would get that out of her. She was one of those women who seem totally without guile. Under other circumstances, he would have found that charming.

In one motion, he slammed the door, grabbed her by the shoulders, and spun her around to face him. Her hands didn't move to cover her breasts. But she covered her eyes, instead, with her lids. "Look at me?"

Emma opened her eyes, looked up at him. "Please? If you don't, he'll know."

Kearney moved his hands down from her shoulders, cupped them under her breasts. He thought of Linda Effingham. And that was stupid, but he loved Linda Effingham, even though she was dead. That had changed nothing for him emotionally. If he didn't make love to this frightened girl, once Montenegro got it out of her Montenegro might think any number of things, but any of them could kill his appearance on national television as the fair-haired boy of the people's revolution.

And he already knew what he was going to deliver there. It had nothing to do with his speech.

Still holding Emma's little breasts, Kearney drew her close to him, bending his face over hers, his lips touching at her mouth. She sank against him like a rag doll. He held her that way, kissing her, not wanting to. Then he swept her up into his arms, and she leaned her head against his chest as he carried her across the room toward his bed.

And Geoffrey Kearney realized something as he removed her clothes, removed his, lay down beside her, began making love to her. She had never known anything like this, was used to the Montenegroes of the world, who demanded and never gave, who substituted force for tenderness. His fingers alone brought her to climax, then again and again.

He slipped between her legs, her body writhing under his. He closed his eyes.

He hadn't wanted it this way at all. Fine. Do it. Be done with it and get the bitch out of the room.

Emma whispered, "Please. Love me?"

Kearney looked away, cursed himself, his job, the world, then looked at little blonde Emma. She was a real blonde. His left hand moved beneath the small of her back, raised her up, his lips touching her neck, his right hand frictioning against her breast.

Her legs wrapped around him, and she began to cry. "All right, Emma. It will be all right."

CHAPTER TEN

Smith struck a match on the hearth, lit his cigar, flicked the match into the flames.

Tonight, Lilly cleaned up the kitchen alone. Normally, he and Wisdom would help. But tonight was an important night for Wisdom, and Smith knew that Lilly Twobears knew that too.

Wisdom sat with the men.

His uncle, Bob Twobears (Lilly's onetime husband had borne the same surname), was speaking. "We'll have to hit the antiaircraft installations simultaneously, and not much before that train goes rolling into Fort Makowski. Otherwise, their normal communications will be our undoing."

Luther Steel nodded. Bill Runningdeer said, "We should figure simultaneous attacks on the antiaircraft installations, while the train is on the way up to the fort. The thing that bugs me is getting out once we get in. We won't have orders or anything to make us look legit. As soon as we're inside, or before, the whole thing could go bang in our faces."

Professor Holden spoke. "I've been giving this a great deal of thought. If Makowski is there, the only reason he's there is to make this an irresistible trap, to spring on us."

"Bravo!" Smith said softly, exhaling cigar smoke.

"I don't understand," Wisdom interrupted. "If you know it's a trap—"

"See, son," Holden began, "we can use that to our advantage. We know that the base commander—"

"Eugene Hackler," Steel supplied. "Armed robbery, murder, rape—may be in on that. When you talked to Rosie, I talked to Clark Pietrowski."

"Pietrowski?" Smith queried.

"Another one of my agents. He got hurt awhile back and was out of commission. He's back on the job now. You'll meet him soon. But he checked up on the name David gave Rosie—"

"That's Detective Shepherd?" Smith asked.

"Right," Holden said.

Steel went on, saying, "She gave the name to Clark, and he got some friendlies in the FBI—people we can still trust —to check. Hackler's typical PSF material, but he's smart, upwardly mobile."

Professor Holden continued then. "We know that this Hackler fellow will be eager to get us inside the fort, so he can spring whatever trap they have. That will work to our advantage. The thing we have to do—and I've been giving that quite a bit of thought—is to make Hackler's—that's his name, Luther?"

Steel nodded.

"We want to make Hackler's trap backfire."

"I'll bite," Smith interjected. "How?"

"We'll load one of the boxcars with explosives, just in case things go wrong. That way, we'll take a lot of them with us. But it was something Bob here said that gave me the idea for how we can turn the tables on them."

Bob Twobears, slightly incredulous sounding, asked, "I said?"

Smith couldn't help but smile.

Holden told them, "All right. Bob, you said your tribe included a number of men who were highly skilled carpenters. You were kind of ticking off a list for me when I asked to know more about your tribe, remember? Anyway, the thing about carpenters sort of sat there. Then when Matthew and Wisdom and Luther and I were watching the fort earlier today, we saw one of the trains. I got to looking at the boxcars. Now, they seem to be made out of some kind of metal, but I remember that some of them have wooden floors. It doesn't matter whether these do or not. We can find that out. But what I'm thinking is that we get the exact dimensions of the boxcars like the train pulls. Your people make an artificial platform out of maybe quarter-inch plywood. We lay it down high enough over the original boxcar floor—we figure out the color and like that beforehand—and we leave enough room underneath for a man and his equipment, a couple of dozen men really, with the gear they'll need. We do that in all of the boxcars except the one we load up with explosives. And the more I think about that, the more I think we'd be better off loading the caboose. That way, we can drop it off once we're out of there, if we get that far, and blow the track and the road behind us.

"But we've got the bulk of our force hidden inside the boxcars under the false floors and out of sight. Once this Hackler character springs his trap, our guys get out of the boxcars at the next opportune moment and we're in."

"The Trojan Horse updated; very good, Dr. Holden," Smith said approvingly.

David Holden smiled. "I always believed a study of the classics was essential."

Smith looked into the flames as they licked upward in the hearth's draft. " '*Arma virumque cano, Troiae qui primus ab oris.* . . . Arms and the man I sing who first from the shores of Troy. . . .' "

CHAPTER ELEVEN

*E*ugene Hackler watched this man who called himself a President.

He was not amused.

Hobart Townes stood beside him. Townes said, "You disapprove."

"Me? No, sir."

President Roman Makowski was being talked through the use of the electrodes by Dr. Masterson. The Marine officer who had been about to give up had apparently found new courage, now stubbornly resisted swearing allegiance to the new President. He was a young lieutenant with about two weeks' growth of beard and heavily bandaged feet. He'd been one of the earliest to arrive and had been subjected to the hosings with icy water on several occasions. He'd given his boots to a female Army officer and, because of that, with only boot socks to protect his feet, had lost one toe on his left foot and two on his right foot.

President Makowski turned the power switch to the lowest position.

Electrodes were attached to the young officer's testicles, nipples, and tongue. The Marine stubbornly resisted letting the current move him. President Makowski very slowly, as if this were something for which he had waited all his life, turned up the dial, increasing the charge.

The young Marine's body began to tremble violently, as if he were in the midst of some sort of fit.

After a little longer than Hackler would have thought prudent, Makowski turned down the current.

A medical technician working with Dr. Masterson pulled on rubber gloves and went over to the Marine, removed the electrode clamped to his tongue. The young officer's tongue was blackened and bleeding.

Dr. Masterson asked, "Will you give it up, son?"

President Makowski said, "All you need to do is come over to my side, boy."

Maybe that was the wrong word because the young Marine officer was black. But whatever, the officer said, "With all due respect—respect to your office, sir—sir—fuck you."

Makowski's face turned several shades of red in rapid succession. "Dr. Masterson, what would happen if the bandages were removed from this man's feet and an additional set of electrodes were installed there?"

Masterson didn't answer for a beat, then, "I, uhh, suppose, Mr. President, it would cause the man very severe pain. But the surgery isn't healed, Mr. President, and it could—"

"I don't really care. Rig it up. I want to see it."

Hackler realized he was balling his hands in and out of fists.

Beside him, Townes whispered almost inaudibly, "You should see some of the women who come out of his bedroom at the White House."

Hackler's eyes flickered to Townes's eyes, then to the eyes of the young Marine officer. This man wouldn't break. "Mr. President, if you'll excuse me, I have duties to attend to."

"No stomach for it, Hacker?"

"It's Hackler, Mr. President. But I do have duties to perform."

"Find me another one after we're finished here. This is interesting."

"I'll ask Dr. Liggett, Mr. President."

"Yeah, you do that, Harper."

Eugene Hackler looked once more at Townes. Townes smiled.

Hackler turned and walked away, a sick feeling in the pit of his stomach. . . .

Dimitri Borsoi watched; there was no facility to listen. Watching two people have sex wasn't exactly something he enjoyed. Montenegro evidently did.

Sitting in a folding chair beside Borsoi, Reefer was evidently getting very excited. "Look at that, Mr. Johnson!"

Borsoi had seen enough.

Ricardo Montenegro scratched at one of the pockmarks on his face, lit a cigarette, but never took his eyes from the television screen. "This Thad Borden is a real stud, huh?"

"Yes," Borsoi agreed politically. "Quite a stud."

"You know, I've never seen Emma respond like that. She's got a lot of potential. When she leaves Borden, bring her over to me, Reefer."

"Yes sir."

Dimitri Borsoi looked at Reefer. Over the time he had known the boy, he'd become quite fond of him in a fatherly way. He recognized Reefer's faults, of course, but saw a certain loyalty there that was more than commendable. He couldn't resist. "Reefer, why are you watching?"

Reefer looked at him. "Mr. Johnson?"

"Why are you watching this? Isn't there one of the girls here you could be with or something?"

"Yeah, but—"

"But?"

"Well, you don't get ta see nothin' like this every day."

"No. That's for certain." Borsoi nodded. He was disappointed. But not in Thad Borden. The young man had all the right qualifications, someone who could handle himself in a fight, was brutal when he had to be, and evidently had quite a bit of charm with the ladies.

That last would help a lot with building his image as the sympathetic leader/spokesman for the Front for the Liberation of North America.

"If we could put this on the television, half the women in this fucking country would be on our side just looking at him," Montenegro enthused.

Borsoi looked at Montenegro's face, said nothing. The eyes were wide, the lips moist looking. Maybe that was why Montenegro beat women with a heavy belt. Maybe he wasn't exactly normal. And Borsoi suddenly wondered who Montenegro watched most closely on the direct video relay: the man or the woman?

Borsoi lit a cigarette, used it as an excuse to look away from the screen. His legs still hurt after the breaks, muscles tightening, spasming.

Someday, Holden would get his.

And maybe this Thad Borden would help in that.

CHAPTER TWELVE

Rose Shepherd sat in the cockpit beside Chester Little. He was his usual garrulous self, saying not a word. She talked anyway. "Long flight out to Colorado, where we change planes, isn't it?"

"Yeah."

"Ever fly a cargo like this, guns and ammunition and stuff?"

"No."

"Why'd you become a pilot."

He shrugged his shoulders, eyes never moving to look at her.

"Flying's always scared me a little," Rose said, looking into the blackness around them. "The part when you're up in the air doesn't bother me, but the takeoffs and landings make me nervous. I guess I'm just always a little spooked, you know? When somebody else is doing the driving, I mean."

He didn't say anything.

"Are you married?" That was a stupid thing to ask him, making her sound like she was on the make.

"Yeah."

"How long?"

"Twelve years."

"Any children?"

"Yeah."

Rose lit a cigarette, exhaled smoke against the windshield. What an answer! "How many?"

"Three."

Well, at least he did something, but sex didn't require all that much in conversational skills. "Boy? Girls?"

"Yeah."

"Well," she almost said "dammit." "How many of each?"

"Two boys, one girl."

"What are their ages?"

"Eleven, nine, seven."

Was he talking in code. "Which are which?"

"Boys are eleven and nine."

She guessed that meant the girl was seven. "Does your wife work?"

"Yeah."

"What's she do?"

"Telephone."

"The telephone company?"

"No."

"Telephone work?"

"Yeah."

"Where'd you learn to fly?"

"Army."

She wanted to ask "Whose army," but she didn't. "How soon will we get there?"

"Two more hours."

"Then we switch planes?"

"Yeah."

"You know the other pilot?"

"Yeah."

"He any good?"

"She."

"She any good?"

"Yeah."

Rose Shepherd was beginning to feel she should have brought a book along. Instead, she stubbed out her cigarette and turned her head toward the side, bunching up her M-65 field jacket like a pillow and resting against the little window behind the vent. Maybe she could make herself go to sleep. . . .

"As we all know from the history we lived, the war itself lasted more than a quarter of a century. But the pivotal point in the war against the Front for the Liberation of North America and its allies in the United States government—such as Roman Makowski and Hobart Townes— came almost twenty-four years ago. The American people at last united behind the Patriot organization, came together, and fought. After the Metro Massacre and the subsequent attack on Fort Makowski, no longer could the average American try to grin and bear it, pretend the violence only affected others, pretend that individual freedoms guaranteed by the Bill of Rights were only temporarily suspended or weren't really that important to begin with. The American people began to realize that freedom of speech, freedom of assembly, freedom from unlawful search and seizure, the right to keep and bear arms—that all of these were, indeed, what the United States was about. And the American people came to realize that the chains of a feudal society based on inequality that their forefathers had immigrated to America in order to throw off were being placed upon them again by a government that no longer wished to represent, but to rule by force.

"Indeed," he went on, "perhaps as human beings we need something to shock us out of our complacency, to make us cry 'Enough!' And that is what happened."

CHAPTER THIRTEEN

*T*he morning was bright and clear and cold. Lem Parrish fingered his Smith & Wesson revolver with his good hand. Getting out of Metro had been insanely dangerous, and deep inside himself he wanted very much never to return there. His wife was safe, and he could join her. He watched the winter-barren trees as the van sped along the two-lane country road.

It actually even smelled free here.

There had never been a time like this. Many times, he'd been disgusted with chasing the news, digging for the truth, and finding slime. But he'd never been so unhappy with his profession.

Too many broadcast and print journalists were just going along with the official government line, that every atrocity was to be laid at the feet of the Patriots, that the Presidential Strike Force personnel were heroes, that the Front for the Liberation of North America might, indeed, be a popular movement working to change America for the good.

"Freedom of speech is one thing, but speaking out against the government in times of crisis such as these should be a criminal offense. We don't have access to secret government strategies, don't even know what the government is saying publicly just to disinform the violence-happy Patriots. So what I'm saying is that we need to stop and think before we open our mouths, and then no one will have to worry about being arrested on suspicion of sedition, and the government can get about its business of making our streets and homes and businesses safe again.

"Granted, search warrants are something to which, as Americans, we have become accustomed. But in order to meet the crisis at hand, extraordinary in nature, extraordinary measures are called for. No, I wouldn't like it if somebody broke down my door in the middle of the night and searched my home. But I don't own a gun, don't have a CB radio, don't have any contraband at all. So what do I have to fear? A little inconvenience, maybe, but the government will pay for a new door. And at least I can sleep more soundly at night knowing my government is using every means possible to get the trigger-happy kill-mongers off the street, to protect my family. Sacrifices have to be made for the collective good.

"With economic times as tough as they are, when was the last time you threw a party for more than six adults? And basically, that's all that's being talked about here. To help us get through this crisis, President Makowski issued an executive order—and very wisely, I think—that any gathering of more than six adults required a simple and easy-to-get permit. You contact the local PSF headquarters in person, by mail, or even by telephone. Request a permit form. It's sent to you with a postage-free return envelope. You answer a couple of questions—names of persons expected to attend, purpose of the event, like that. And that's all. Then mail it in, remembering to keep the duplicate copy of the permit for yourself. It's automatically approved. But what you get in return is the peace of mind from knowing that unauthorized meetings—like Patriot Cell training sessions, gang meetings, things like that—can more easily be detected, prevented, broken up, and that violators can now easily be placed behind bars, taken off the streets, making the streets safer for you and your family. A temporary measure, sure, but necessary. I, for one, would be happy to see such a measure kept in force after the crisis is under control. It would be a solid legal weapon for combating the growing drug problem and keeping down street violence. Let's hear it for President Makowski.

"Guns have no place in today's society, except in the hands of the police and the military. And wouldn't it be wonderful, someday, if America could be like England, where even the police don't need to carry guns? In Japan, of course, guns have been illegal for a long time, and that nation's crime rate and especially the murder rate are so low every American should hang his head in shame. Just because a minority of men get some sort of psychosexual high out of murdering defenseless animals and birds doesn't mean there's any special right guaranteed to them to take their instruments of destruction into the street and kill. But that's what has been happening, isn't it? I applaud President Makowski's recently introduced bill that will make the possession of a contraband firearm or any type of knife designed for other than kitchen or work-related use with a blade in excess of three inches punishable by a mandatory fine of $25,000 per count and a minimum of five years in prison. This is the sort of tough legislation we've needed for decades. So what that the founding fathers put in an amendment about being armed in the militia. In those days, there were wild Indians, like the Apaches and the Sioux and the Comanche to worry about. Maybe ordinary people having access to guns was okay two hundred years ago, but this isn't the Wild West anymore, and the tens of thousands of deliberate murders committed every year with Saturday night specials, assault guns, and automatic shotguns have got to stop sometime. President Makowski is the first President in history to stand up to the gun-nut lobbyists and tell the NRA and the Second Amendment Foundation where to go. That's the kind of courage we need in America today, the kind of courage that doesn't need a bazooka to back it up."

Journalists. He could have recited dozens more print and electronic media editorials that were just as inane and just as frightening. Lem Parrish sighed. Patsy Alfredi sat beside him behind the wheel. "What's bugging you, Lem?"

"I was just thinking what a crazy job I've got, that's all. I try to tell the truth, so people can make up their minds for themselves. But there are so damn many lies."

"That just means you should keep telling the truth, then, doesn't it?"

Parrish shook his head and smiled. He was outnumbered. When the American people heard the same reprocessed lies over and over from almost everyone in media and only heard the truth from a few underground newspapers or radio stations that had to keep on the move, how could they be expected to tell truth from lies? If you heard a lie often enough, after a while didn't it begin to sound true?

"I'll tell you, Lem, you're bitter."

"Boy, how'd you figure that out, Patsy?"

She didn't laugh. "My husband and son, remember?"

Her husband had been a policeman killed by the FLNA, Parrish remembered, her son a serviceman who, along with dozens of anonymous others, had died during an FLNA firebombing. "So how do you do it?"

"Make myself wake up every morning instead of slashing my wrists?" He didn't know what to say to that. "It's easy, really," Patsy went on. "I tell myself that if I don't keep fighting, the bastards who murdered my family win. If I do keep fighting, I'm showing them they can't get away with it, that people still care and aren't gonna quit just because they're scared of dying."

"I'm scared of dying."

"Hell, we all are, Lem. What I wanna do is make them scared, the FLNA, the PSF. So maybe some other woman won't have to lose her husband and her son. You understand what I mean?"

Parrish nodded. A man of words all his life, he had none now. . . .

"I am the Vindicator, the leader of the Front for the Liberation of North America. But I lead in the name of oppressed peoples here and everywhere who fight for freedom and economic and social justice. Too long has this so-called United States raped the poor and lowly to line the pockets of the rich and powerful. Oppressed peoples everywhere have had enough of this joke called America." Geoffrey Kearney looked at Borsoi and Montenegro. Montenegro had been looking at him strangely all day. "So how was that, Mr. Johnson?"

"Very good, I thought, Thad."

"Esta bien, amigo! Much feeling. I like that."

"The one thing, don't you agree, Ricardo," Borsoi said, standing up, shaking his legs a little, then lighting a cigarette, "is I'm still getting a little less conviction than I would like. These are words you have to speak from the heart, Thad. How are you coming with the memorization?"

"Real good. Hey, I wanted to say thanks for sendin' Emma along last night, you know? I was down in the dumps and everything, but she really picked me up."

Ricardo Montenegro laughed. "Did you pick her up, too?" And Montenegro grinned, evidently waiting for a response.

Kearney, in his best American accent, said, "Hey, yeah, stirred things up a little anyways," and he tried a leering grin.

Evidently the grin worked. Montenegro slapped his right knee. "When you are leading this pis-ant country, we'll get you all the girls you want; you can wear out your pecker, *muchacho!*"

Borsoi smiled good-naturedly. It was an odd relationship between Borsoi and Montenegro, Kearney thought. There was obvious disapproval on Borsoi's part, and obvious disregard for anything on the part of Montenegro. Borsoi said, "Let's hear some more of your speech, Thad."

"Right, Mr. Johnson." Kearney cleared his throat, shifted his feet a little, began reading again. "The FLNA, as we're called—"

" '. . . as we are called,' Thad."

"Right, Mr. Johnson. The FLNA, as we are called, has only one goal, and that goal is the liberation of the American people. That goal will be accomplished by the following steps." Kearney cleared his throat again.

"Like some water?" Montenegro asked.

"No thanks, Mr. Montenegro, just all these words, you know."

"They'll come easily to you when you deliver your address, Thad." Borsoi smiled knowingly.

Kearney nodded, continuing, ". . . following steps: the capture and disarming of the murderous organization that calls itself the Patriots; the abolishment of current United States currency; the eventual redistribution of wealth and property on an equal basis to all Americans."

"Now, remember, there will be specific questions asked by the reporters on the panel up there on the stage with you. We have all the questions in advance, of course," Borsoi told him, "and one of those questions will deal with the plan for redistribution. Pretend I've just asked you that question. Have you memorized the answer yet?"

"Almost, Mr. Johnson, but I got it written down right here."

"Fine, read me the answer then."

Kearney thumbed through his notes as clumsily as he could without looking too obvious. Then he read the answer to the question. "Yes, Mr. Bailey, I'm very glad you asked me to clarify that point. First of all, by abolishing current United States currency, all those who are hoarding large sums of cash will be left with worthless paper and forced to redeem it for the new devalued currency or be without currency at all. Now, for a very short time—and let me emphasize the word 'very'—there will be hardship for the average little guy out there. But very soon after that—and again, let me emphasize the word 'very'—each family and individual in the United States—or as we hope it will someday be called, the People's Democratic Republic of North America, encompassing all of what today is the United States, Canada, and Mexico—will be given a government allotment, a new start toward finacial security and independence."

Borsoi said, "Then Lawrence Pilsner—you've probably watched his evening news show—will ask you about what will happen to the U.S. currency that is turned in. We've intentionally made certain that's asked about because there will be a lot of skeptics out there, so we'll give them an answer that will alleviate their doubts. Can you find that answer and read it for us, Thad?"

"Yes, sir." Again, Kearney thumbed through his notes. As he did, he lit a cigarette.

Borsoi said, "Remember, don't light up on television. Smoking is socially frowned on, and you want to have a clean public image, right?"

"Gotcha, Mr. Johnson. Here it is!" He found his preprinted spontaneous response. "I'm glad you asked, Mr. Pilsner, because I'm certain that a number of viewers are concerned about that. At first, the redistribution of wealth will be accomplished through government scrip, and that's for a very good reason. We will keep the U.S. currency as is for overseas trade for a short period. This will allow the People's Democratic Republic of North America to honor previously made international debt." It was obvious to Kearney what was really intended. Collect all the money, dump it on the international currency market at a low price for gold or Swiss francs, then devalue. Economic chaos for everyone else while the rulers of this new "Democratic Republic" would become multibillionaires virtually overnight.

Borsoi asked, "Thad, there'll be a question concerning the name of the new country. Can you skip over to that?"

"Sure thing." Kearney found it, inhaled smoke, began to read. "Why do we call it a name that sounds Communist when Communist regimes around the world are crumbling? Well, it may sound Communist, but it isn't, let me assure you. I'm talking democracy, in the purest and most traditional sense of the word, and a government that is run by the people, one that is an auton—"

"What is it, Thad?" Borsoi asked.

"How do you say this word?"

He started to show the printout to Borsoi, but Borsoi only smiled good-naturedly. "The word is 'autonomous,' Thad. It means 'self-governing,' okay?"

"Aw-tan-e-mus."

"Right."

Kearney nodded, saying, ". . . one that is an au-tonomous republic. That's all the name implies, that's all the name is. And of course, the people could change the name if they wished, because they will run the country."

Geoffrey Kearney had a bang-up finale planned for the television show.

CHAPTER FOURTEEN

O'Brien said to him, "Mr. Kaminsky, are you sure?"

"How difficult can it be?"

O'Brien shrugged his shoulders. "A revolver's pretty simple, but so was—"

"That automatic the last time was for crazy people."

O'Brien took off his dark-lensed glasses and tossed his cigarette butt on the ground. "Fine. Here's what you do. This is a Smith & Wesson Model 686. With .38 Special plus Ps in it, there's virtually no felt recoil to speak of." O'Brien was taking out the middle of the gun. "This latch is the cylinder release catch, and when you push it forward, the cylinder swings out—this is the cylinder. Now, when it's empty like this, you just load in the cartridges."

"The bullets; I understand that."

O'Brien only nodded.

Ralph Kaminsky would have thought the Metro SWAT team commander would have known more about guns than this. "Where are the extra bullets?"

"You mean the spares, the—"

"The extra bullets, of course."

"In those pouches on your belt. I kept it nice and simple. You open the flap on the pouch and the pouch falls outward —it's called a hinged dump box—and you just grap the—

the extra bullets. But you have to remove the empty cases from the cylinder first."

"What empty cases?"

"After the bullets are fired, the cases remain. You punch them out by pushing on this ejector rod, like this," and O'Brien stabbed a thin metal rod poking out from the thing in the middle he'd taken out into the palm of his gloved left hand several times. "All you've gotta do, Mr. Kaminsky. Let the empties fall onto the ground, load the fresh ones in, and then close the cylinder back into the frame. All you have to do is pull the trigger here. Don't worry about cocking the hammer. But you'll be with us, sir, and the Presidential Strike Force personnel will be between us and the Patriots—"

"I wish you wouldn't call them that."

"Patriots? But that's their name, sir."

"It doesn't matter; it makes them sound like they're, like they're patriotic or something."

O'Brien handed him the gun, and Kaminsky took it. Then O'Brien handed him six bullets. He took them, trying to remember how to open the thing in the middle of the gun. He pushed on the switch-shaped thing on the gun's left side and tried shaking the middle thing out. O'Brien said, "You have to push it out, sir." Kaminsky pushed it out, but almost dropped the bullets. He loaded them, one at a time. As he started to close the thing up, the bullets started to fall out. O'Brien helped catch them. "You can't turn the revolver upside down, sir. You have to keep the muzzle— that's the front of the barrel—pointed at the ground."

Kaminsky said nothing, but did as O'Brien said, and the bullets didn't fall out this time when he closed up the gun. He decided against putting it in the holster, kept it in his hand instead.

The PSF officer—a Captain Carlsberg—was talking to

some of his people up closer to the road. Kaminsky said to O'Brien, "Let's go talk to them and see what they're up to."

"Yes, sir. Please keep your finger off the trigger, sir, because the ground's very uneven and there could be an accidental discharge if you were to slip and accidentally pull the trigger."

What did O'Brien think he was, anyway? Kaminsky took his finger off the trigger rather than argue it. More of this macho guy gun crap, he thought.

The ground was rough and uneven in the clearing, and he was careful of his footing.

As he and O'Brien approached Captain Carlsberg, the PSF officer turned, his eyes riveting to Kaminsky's hand. "Isn't that a little jumping the gun, if y'all know what I mean?"

Kaminsky looked at the gun, put it away in the holster. The damned thing didn't fit properly, he realized. "How soon before the two enemy units come together, Captain?"

"Should be about another fifteen minutes. Our informant inside Metro intercepted another of their communications. Parrish and those other scum from inside the city are on the way, and we know that Diamond and the ones outside the city are on their way too. Got us an observation post on a road they frequent. Just saw 'em pass."

"Are Holden and that Shepherd woman with them? The damn bitch traitor!"

"We don't know, Mr. Kaminsky. If we're lucky. If we ain't, well, we ain't, but we got us some ways o' makin' any we get hold of alive tell us anything they know, so maybe we'll find their base camp anyways."

"You sound like a thorough man, Captain. And somehow, I can't help but think we've met before. I can tell, if you don't mind my saying so, that you're from around

Metro, the way you talk, I mean, such a charming way of talking."

Captain Carlsberg laughed. "O'Brien here should recognize me, but I never seen y'all."

Beside Kaminsky, O'Brien took a sudden step forward. "Harrelston? Sam Harrelston?"

Carlsberg laughed. "God, y'all's got a good memory. Five years ago."

"You were a private in the Army then, and there was this woman—"

"That bitch." Carlsberg laughed. "Too bad y'all's SWAT team fellas nailed her 'fore I blew her fuckin' brains out."

And then Carlsberg turned away, and when Kaminsky looked at O'Brien, O'Brien's face was white and the vein in his right temple was pulsing. . . .

"We could've found this place, you know, Patsy. You didn't have to risk coming into Metro and then driving out with us. I mean, we're not taking a Sunday drive in the park or anything."

"I've got a niece in Metro, Lem, and I've been meaning to see her for a while. This farm where we're making the transfer isn't too easy to locate. Don't worry about it. If I didn't get out of camp every once in a while, I'd go whacko."

"I know what you mean, not about the camp, but just getting away."

"I figure, if we fight hard and plan well, maybe there'll be peace by the time somebody's grandchildren start growing up. And that's on the optimistic side, Lem, because once we win—talk about optimistic—"

Parrish laughed out loud.

"Once we do win," Patsy went on, "It's gonna take years rooting out all the people in government who were on the FLNA side and all the Presidential Strike Force is a lot of hooligans—heavily armed hooligans—and they're not gonna turn in their arms and go to jail, where they came from. There could be bands of them roaming the countryside for the next twenty years."

"Do you ever wonder, maybe, if we're just fighting evolution?" There, he'd said it, something that had been troubling him since God knows when.

Patsy's voice dropped. "What do you mean?"

"Are we just anachronisms, living relics, like a dinosaur at the opera or something? Is this just the way mankind is going, and all we're doing is fighting the tide of inevitability?"

"You mean, everything would sort of naturally get screwed up?"

"No, well, yeah, but what I mean is, are we kidding ourselves when we say we're fighting to restore freedom? I mean, maybe is it just that people these days don't want to be bothered enough to be free, just rather be comfortable with not having to make any decisions, let their lives be run for them? Is freedom too much trouble?"

"If I thought that—I mean, I've thought about that—but if I believed that, I think I'd slash my wrists."

Parrish shrugged his shoulders. . . .

Myra was a pretty woman. While Clark and Tom and Randy slept in the back of the plane with the cargo, just like they had when they had flown them from Metro to Colorado, Rose sat in the cockpit again. "So how's it going for David and everybody? You know you can't say a lot over the radio."

"There's this huge fort? I mean, it's like something out of *Star Wars* or something, all fortified and high tech and everything. That's where they've got all the officers they kidnapped. And David and Luther and this guy Matthew

Smith—neat fella, but he's spoken for, this real pretty Indian woman named Lilly?—well, they all figure the only way in is to steal a train and then fight their way out. Scares the crap outta me thinking about it."

Rose stared downward. There were no clouds, except high above, and she could see the mountainous terrain below them in scary detail. Ridges of granite, and between the ridges gray white that was snow. Streams and rivers that were blue-black ribbons wound between the ridges. And sometimes there would be a deep dished-out valley and sometimes mountains that spiked upward so abruptly she had to convince herself the mountain wouldn't puncture the skin of the aircraft.

They were terrain following, which was slow, required terrific concentration on the part of the pilot—Myra seemed to be a good one, thank God—and made for a bumpy ride. Unlike commercial flights, there was always turbulence, always a feeling of motion. She tried not thinking about her stomach and secretly envied Clark and the other two men that they could sleep. . . .

Geoffrey Kearney unloaded the Smith & Wesson 5906's chamber, then replaced the magazine. The magazine was full, thirteen rounds.

He stood in front of the mirror, rehearsing.

Not his speech.

He reached under the sports coat he wore, sweeping the pistol around and on target and pulled the trigger, wheeled about forty-five degrees right and pulled the trigger again, then ninety degrees left, pulling the trigger, but never once raising the semiautomatic pistol high enough to use the sights, merely looking across it and point shooting instead.

He replaced the pistol inside the waistband of his trousers at the small of his back, stood there a moment, then drew, repeating the drill, going for as much fluidity as he could muster.

It would have to be very quick if he had any hope of making it through alive. And he wasn't certain of the seating arrangement for Borsoi and Montenegro, so he didn't really know his exact fields of fire.

Kearney tried again, this time firing to the extreme left as he dipped into a crouch, then behind him to the extreme right.

He tried to remember everything he'd ever learned from the older, more experienced men in SIS, everything he'd learned from the nail-hard Special Air Service personnel he'd sometimes trained with, everything he'd learned in his years in the field.

He'd killed before in the line of duty, and sometimes he thought too often. But no job was ever as important as this, and he realized that if, somehow, he made it through, no job would ever be that important again.

He put the pistol under his coat, tried again. He'd start from a hammer down double-action mode, of course, so on subsequent shots the trigger pull would be lighter. He tried to compensate for that, but couldn't cock the hammer for his subsequent shots because teaching himself to waste that amount of time by performing what would be, with ammunition, unnecessary, could be fatal to his timing.

He changed his drill, going to double taps, and as he went into the draw, he stomped his right foot hard to settle his bone structure and give a more rigid firing platform.

He'd seen Israelis, security people, who were very good. He'd worked with them a time or two.

Eyes always on the target, everything otherwise by rote, just the same every time. That could be good, unless something totally untrained for arose. He didn't want that. What if Borsoi pulled that Glock he wore in time to fire back?

Kearney tried varying the drill as much as he could. He realized that he was being watched on video, but he was supposed to be a streetwise tough, supposed to be someone who lived by violence. And he had to risk it, needed the practice if he would succeed.

Borsoi's Glock-17 was a wild card, certainly, because of all semiautomatic pistols commonly encountered it was among the fastest for a first shot, and inherently quite accurate. And Kearney didn't doubt for a moment that Borsoi was very good at killing people.

Kearney kept practicing. . . .

Mitch Diamond realized something was wrong and had been wrong for several miles. He should have reacted sooner, he told himself.

They were being followed in a very loose, almost informal way, but followed nonetheless. He said to young Dave Winters sitting beside him, "Remember that hand signal I showed you?"

"Yeah. So?"

"So make it out the passenger window."

"You mean we're breaking up the convoy?"

"Damn right, Dave." Diamond picked up his CB microphone. If he was being followed, there was a good chance that Lem Parrish and Patsy Alfredi and the inner-city Patriot Cell were in trouble, too. "This is Talk-Talk to Concrete Kids, Talk-Talk to Concrete Kids. Come back."

Nothing came back. Even with the boosters he had provided on the CBs used by the Patriots, the range was still too great.

He took the side road and turned off. "Damn!"

CHAPTER FIFTEEN

*H*e'd opted to be in the front lines, and for some reason O'Brien was up there with him. Probably trying to hog all the glory for himself, Kaminsky mused. On his right was Captain Carlsberg. Ralph Kaminsky realized full well that the men and women of the Presidential Strike Force were all former prisoners in federal and military penitentiaries, but O'Brien's anger seemed to him totally unfounded. After all, it only stood to reason that the PSF people were picked because they were rehabilitated and could be counted on.

Carlsberg was on the radio, something about the convoy from Metro coming in, but the convoy from the Patriot Camp outside Metro eluding the vehicle following it. "You fuckin' asshole. When I get my hands on ya, ya'll wish you was never born!" Carlsberg threw down his radio. "So we lost the weapons, but it looks like they wasn't able to alert the others, and they're on their way, about five minutes or less out."

"I've been thinking, Captain Carlsberg," Kaminsky said, "that I ought to attempt to make the arrest. I have a bull-horn right here and—"

"We start shootin', and anybody left alive that we figure might give us some good shit on the Patriots we put the screws to, and the rest of 'em we waste. Arrest my ass, Mr. Kaminsky."

Kaminsky shook his head, blinked. "But you can't shoot wounded people who aren't resisting. That's—"

"That's what it is." Carlsberg grinned.

Beside Kaminsky, O'Brien almost growled. "You're a damn animal, Carlsberg, or whatever you're callin' yourself."

"This is war, O'Brien, not roustin' some drunk college brats on Saturday night. And we can't take anymore prisoners than we's got already. Ya'll don't like it, get the hell out. Otherwise, ya'll better be shootin' along with the rest o' us, see?" And Carlsberg gestured with the gun in his hand.

For a split second, Kaminsky thought O'Brien would go for his gun. . . .

Mitch Diamond got on the sideband again, saying, "Stay with me. I got the amorous lover. Execute." He hung up the microphone. His "amorous lover" was a green station wagon about a half mile back, the same vehicle that he'd spotted following them, and he imagined packed with PSF. His radio message had been a simple one. The rest of the vehicles in his convoy were to turn off, come after him, trapping the pursuit vehicle between them, except for the vehicles carrying the weapons, which by now would already be returning to camp via an alternate route. Two hundred assault rifles, ten thousand rounds of ammunition, explosive ordnance, radio equipment, and, oddly, one of the most vital items, combat boots, could not be lost; replacing any or all of the equipment would be next to impossible.

David's father-in-law, Thomas Ashbrooke, and Ashbrooke's Israeli friends were smuggling ordnance in along the Florida and Georgia coast, at least two shipments a week, using the old drug routes, but the amount of equipment their small, fast boats could bring in while trying to evade the Coast Guard patrols that were now PSF controlled was just too little. Eventually, maybe a year from now, the volume would be high enough to have more than a negligible effect.

But now, the stuff Rosie had boosted out of that Delta Force underground facility was like gold.

More valuable than gold, really.

Lots of firearms were in the black market, military stuff the PSF would steal out of their own stores and sell for cash only, M-16s going for five thousand dollars apiece with one magazine and a box of twenty rounds of military 5.56mm Ball. Heckler & Koch guns, used by some of the more elite PSF units, were fetching close to ten thousand dollars.

Even if the money had been available, lining the pockets of the PSF just to get one extra weapon would have been immoral.

He picked up the CB microphone again, saying, "Concrete Kids, this is Talk-Talk calling. Come back. You're riding into a trap."

Static. They were still too far off, or maybe the trap had already been sprung.

Mitch Diamond blinked back a tear. He'd never really gotten around to telling Patsy Alfredi that he thought she was very special. "Damn," Diamond hissed, his throat tight.

Beside him, Winters asked, "What?"

"I missed a great opportunity, kid. Dammit."

He saw the green station wagon again.

When it came time to spring the little trap on them, he hoped they all fought back really hard so there'd be moral justification for killing them. Unlike the PSF, the Patriots didn't usually kill people who'd already given up.

CHAPTER SIXTEEN

*T*here were three trucks following a solitary van, the trucks large enough, the kind people used when they moved themselves rather than hiring professional movers, rental trucks, painted bright yellow with the name of the company that had rented them painted on the sides.

Kaminsky drew the handgun from the holster on his right hip. He remembered his last experience with a handgun, told himself he should have kept his gloves on.

To his right, Captain Carlsberg had an M-16 rifle. Talk about complicated! Kaminsky thought. O'Brien, at Kaminsky's left, had a handgun.

Nervous, Kaminsky needed to talk. "What kind of gun is that, O'Brien?"

O'Brien looked faintly amazed, then whispered back, "Walther P-88, 9mm."

"I see." Kaminsky nodded. That wasn't a name he'd ever heard of, but he remembered that a 9mm was the kind of gun he'd hurt his hand on the last time. Almost unconscious of the action until it was performed, he edged away a little from O'Brien.

Carlsberg was talking into his radio. "When they turn off the road just past the fence, but wait until the last vehicle is past the fence, hear? Then ya'll's men with the LAW rockets trash that road 'hind them." He threw down the radio set.

Kaminsky watched the van, watched it pass the fence,

watched the first of the four rental trucks follow it, then the second, then the third, at last the fourth.

There was a whooshing sound followed in the next instant by a terrifically loud explosion, and the road behind the last truck seemed to go up in smoke.

Captain Carlsberg opened fire with his rifle. Kaminsky pointed his handgun at the van in the lead, tried aiming it for the windshield, scrinched his eyes almost shut as he pushed the gun away from him and pulled on the trigger.

It was hard to make it move.

He worked his finger up higher along the trigger, drew the trigger all the way back, and the gun seemed to explode. Kaminsky's ears rang, and hot metal from the rifle beside him was flying everywhere, pieces of hot metal from O'Brien's damn 9mm thing getting down inside the front of Kaminsky's jacket.

There was a terrific pain in Kaminsky's right-hand first finger, and as he looked, he realized that the trigger of the handgun was pinching his flesh and his finger was stuck. He held the gun by the front, tried pulling his hand free, blood spurting out of his finger.

Carlsberg screamed at him, "Point that fuckin' gun at the damn enemy, Kaminsky, not my face, hear!"

Kaminsky tried pulling the trigger farther back, but it didn't want to go farther back, and his finger really hurt now, blood again.

Another explosion.

One of the trucks blew up.

There was so much gunfire all around him that Kaminsky couldn't think straight.

In desperation, he pulled his finger away from the gun, and he shouted with the pain, "Aww!" His finger was covered with blood.

A man and a woman were running from the van, its tires

shot out and the vehicle smoking, as if it were about to catch fire. The woman was limping badly, as if she'd been shot in the leg or something. Kaminsky let his gun fall to the ground, trying to get his handkerchief out of his pocket with his left hand, but that was very awkward because the handkerchief was in his right-front pocket and the damn holster covered the pocket. He tried turning the belt around on his waist to get the holster away.

The woman fell down. The man—it looked like he could only use one hand—it was that meddling radio commentator Lem Parrish!—fired a little gun in his hand toward a half-dozen PSF personnel rushing him.

One of the PSF men went down, dead or wounded. Kaminsky's finger stung like a bad tooth. The other five PSF men fired, the woman shooting at them as the whole front of Parrish's shirt turned red with blood and he crumpled to the ground, the woman catching a faceful of bullets and falling down dead beside him.

Kaminsky at last had his handkerchief.

The volume of gunfire suddenly increased, and there was another explosion, and Kaminsky clamped his hands over his ears, blood and all.

And then everything stopped. There was a hollow sound in his ears, like waves rushing in off the ocean. Kaminsky looked around. There was a lot of shouting. Carlsberg and O'Brien were running. Kaminsky picked up his dropped gun with his left hand and stood up, climbed up over the embankment, nearly dropped his handkerchief, ran after them.

The battle was over.

It looked like three of the people from Metro were still alive, at least two of them bleeding heavily.

Plastic restraints were wrapped around their wrists. They were thrown down to the ground.

Captain Carlsberg put his rifle to a woman's head. "Where is the Patriot Camp outside Metro? We know the location of the Patriot Camp inside the city. It's being destroyed right now, and the rest of you bastards are dying. Where's the other camp, hear!"

The woman's mouth was bleeding, and she spit out teeth. It looked like somebody had hit her. She couldn't have been more than twenty, Kaminsky realized.

"Where!" And Carlsberg jabbed the front of his rifle where the bullets came out into her right ear, twisted it. She fell facedown, and he dropped on top of her back, still twisting the rifle into her ear. Blood started pouring out.

O'Brien snapped, "You fucking animal!"

Carlsberg looked up at him.

O'Brien was pointing his gun at Captain Carlsberg.

Kaminsky stepped away because watching what was happening to the girl was making him sick to his stomach.

Carlsberg stood up. "Ya'll bracin' me, motherfucker?"

O'Brien almost snarled. "I hate these people as much as you do, but they're citizens of the United States, and they have a right to a trial, dammit!"

Captain Carlsberg smiled, said, "I guess ya'll's right, man. I got carried away." He took his rifle out of the girl's ear, started to turn away.

O'Brien holstered his handgun and reached down toward the girl, murmuring, "You have the right to remain silent—"

Kaminsky started to tell O'Brien that the Miranda rule had been suspended, but then Captain Carlsberg wheeled around and shot O'Brien in the back with the M-16, the bullets seeming to shred through O'Brien, ripping his clothes and blood spraying everywhere.

The girl screamed as O'Brien fell on top of her.

Then Carlsberg looked at Kaminsky. "Ya'll got anythin' to say?"

"No—no, Captain."

Captain Carlsberg kicked O'Brien's body off the girl's body, then hauled her up to her knees. "Want what he got, bitch? Where's the damn camp!"

She looked up at Captain Carlsberg, told him, "I don't know, but if I did, I'd rather die than tell." And then she spit blood out of her mouth, just missing Captain Carlsberg's face. Carlsberg stepped back and shot her in the head, her body just flopping over on top of O'Brien's.

Gone were thoughts of the pain in his finger. His bowels felt loose.

Ralph Kaminsky turned away, walked, stumbled, fell. As he looked, he was face to face with Lem Parrish. Only Lem Parrish was dead, of course.

But there was something in those wide open eyes that scared Ralph Kaminsky more than the blood and gore and death.

There was a look of righteousness there.

Kaminsky threw up.

CHAPTER SEVENTEEN

David Holden swung down out of the Suburban's front seat, Matthew Smith doing the same from the driver's side.

Holden glanced at the Rolex Sea-Dweller on his left wrist. "About five minutes if they're still running on time," he announced to Smith.

The truck that would haul away the weapons and matériel aboard the aircraft pulled up in the snow a short distance behind them.

Holden walked toward the front of the Suburban. The sun was low on the horizon, a winter sun nearing dusk. But there was an almost total absence of wind, and the snow seemed to insulate them somehow. Holden didn't bother zipping up his M-65 field jacket, nor with his gloves, instead just pushing back the skirts of his coat and thrusting his hands into his trouser pockets.

Smith lit a cigar, the first Holden had seen him smoke all day. "You're not at all addicted, are you?"

"What? To smoking? Hardly. If I were, it would cease to be a thing of enjoyment, wouldn't it. I was going to say that I've been admiring your knife. Might I see it?"

Holden told him, "Sure," then reached under his right armpit with his right hand and undid the snaps of the inverted sheath, then pulled the blade from the leather. He handed it to Smith butt forward.

Smith took it carefully and slowly. " 'The Defender'—
how appropriate a name for your knife, Professor."

Holden didn't know what to say.

"Hollow handle, of course, flat grind, I see. Excellent. A
Crain knife, I see. Jack Crain, isn't it?" Holden nodded. "If
this war ever ends, I'll have to contact Mr. Crain and ask
him to make me one like this, if you'd have no objection, of
course."

"None whatsoever," Holden told him. "Let me ask you a
question," he said as Smith returned the Defender knife.
"Why do you carry that little .25 automatic?"

Smith thumbed his hat back from his forehead, his face
seaming with laughter as he made the little Beretta appear
almost magically from inside his waistband. He seemed to
weigh it in his hand. "I discovered some time ago that persons love feeling self-satisfied, and for some persons that
translates to a feeling of power over others. So if I'm in a
situation where trying to get my primary ordnance into play
is awkward, I use this. On occasion, when I've let someone
get the drop on me, discarding the 92F here," and he patted
the black leather full-flap holster at his right hip with the
full-size 9mm Beretta in it, which was identical to Holden's
own, "throwing my gun down has imparted to my adversary
that momentary feeling of power through superiority. Then,
too, the .25 has helped me to turn the tables and survive.
The 950 BS is accurate, lightweight, all but invisible when
worn properly and, of greatest importance, exceedingly reli-
able, yet very small."

"You seem quite the student of gunfighting, Smith."

Smith made the little black .25 automatic disappear, took
his cigar from his teeth, seemed to study its glowing tip. "I
suppose one might say that, but I've always considered that
the most practical skill any person could develop was that
which allowed him or her to stay alive. All other skills, if

death comes, are, of course, lost. What does it profit a man to eschew the most basic tenets of self-defense, hence self-preservation, while at the same time bending every effort toward the development of some crucially needed skill, such as surgery, teaching, the arts? And then all that diligence spent in study, in perfecting one's abilities, is lost to oneself and the world at large because someone who never bothered to exercise his humanity at all takes it into his head to kill? How many Pasteurs and Curies, Delacroixs and Dalis, Dickinsons and Shakespeares, Einsteins and Darwins have been lost to the world because they couldn't do such a relatively simple thing as guard their own lives? I think too many.

"Certainly," Smith went on, exhaling cigar smoke as he talked, "I wouldn't compare myself with men and women such as these, but each human life is of equal importance because it is of supreme importance to its possessor among those who value themselves. Have I studied gunfighting? Indeed. I have always had a great interest in firearms, as a pastime and as a passion. When shooting for practice, one competes only against oneself; when shooting in sport or in those rare instances of life and death, one competes against others. Yet in the final analysis, it's the self that makes the difference, the most worthy opponent."

"Do you ever give a short answer to a question, Smith?" David Holden laughed.

Smith smiled, said, "Sometimes."

From behind them, there was a sound, and Holden turned to the east. A spot on the horizon only, it was the plane. . . .

She watched Myra's hands as they seemed to glide over the controls of the aircraft with a will of their own. More to reassure herself than from genuine curiosity, Rose Shepherd asked, "How long have you been doing this? I mean, you look like you really know this stuff blindfolded."

"Pretty long time. I've always loved flying. You're nervous, aren't you, Rosie?"

Myra had picked up the "Rosie" bit from David and Luther and Bill, Rose realized. "Yeah, I'm a little nervous. You kind of feel flying more this way."

"You do at that; that's why I love it. Years ago, I had a chance to fly for one of the airlines, not one of the real big ones, but a substantial one, you know? Well, I thought about it and everything. Looking sharp with my pilot's uniform and everything, the whole works. Well, I decided I didn't want to do that. It was better to really fly."

Rose was still watching Myra's hands. "What are you doing now?"

"I'm lowering the landing gear; we're well into our final approach. I can see Smith's Suburban, over there," and Myra gestured off to the right of the snowy field for which they were heading.

Rose saw David.

"Rosie, don't you worry. I've landed in lots yuckier-looking fields than this; this'll be a piece of cake."

"Right."

"You've always gotta remember the old line about good landings."

"Good landings?" Rosie asked.

"Yeah. 'Any landing you can walk away from is a good landing.' " Myra laughed.

"Right. Tell you what. When we go against that Fort Makowski—"

"Yeah?"

"Well, you stick right with me when the bad guys start shooting at us. There's an old line about any gunfight you can walk away from being a good gunfight."

Myra laughed. "Touché. We'll be on the ground in about forty-five seconds. Hang in there, Rosie."

Rose's hands were white knuckled on the armrests of the copilot's seat. And her eyes focused on the second yoke; it wiggled around, moved, as if invisible hands guided it.

Rose looked over it, focusing tight on the Suburban, on David, who was walking away from the car, toward the field where the aircraft would be touching down in—

Rose Shepherd felt the first bump, then a lurch, her stomach feeling it hardest of all, then another bump, then another bump, and she realized they were down, the aircraft taxiing over the snow-packed ground, Myra seeming to have perfect control, the plane bouncing, jumping.

And suddenly, it stopped.

Myra told her, "Pull that handle and watch out for the props when you get out."

Rose looked at her, smiled, worked the door handle with one hand and her seat restraint with the other.

She threw open the wing door, her legs a little wobbly from sitting so long, from the landing, from seeing David. He was walking toward the aircraft.

The cold air stung her cheeks. She told herself millions of women spent big bucks to get that kind of a blushed look in their faces.

She started to climb down.

David started running.

She jumped down, fell to her knees, stood up, ran.

David took her into his arms, kissed her, said, "God, I love you, Rosie."

Rose Shepherd wanted to tell him about the baby. Instead, she told him something equally as important and easier to handle. "I never missed anybody so much in my life, David."

He held her, kissed her, held her. Her arms were tight

around his waist, and she let his mouth move across her face.

She'd died and gone to heaven, she told herself. But it didn't matter, so long as she was with David.

Rose Shepherd closed her eyes, tried forgetting that she wore two guns and a knife, combat boots, what amounted to a man's battle uniform. She just let David touch her hair, kiss her face, hold her tight.

Heaven or the other place, so long as she was with David and he loved her forever. That was all that mattered.

CHAPTER EIGHTEEN

Rose Shepherd helped Lilly Twobears in the kitchen.

The cabin—it was large, comfortable—was beautiful, the sort of place she'd always hoped someday she would live in, snow-laden pine trees everywhere, a spring nearby that was partially frozen over, but in the spring would make those funny noises like the babbling brooks in fairy tales.

And Lilly Twobears was perfect for the place. Long, gorgeously beautiful hair, so straight and healthy looking, so shiny. She was feminine is a very natural, comfortable way, her smile, her alto voice, her pretty dark eyes.

And Rose Shepherd felt a little awkward.

When they had come to the cabin, driven there by the somewhat enigmatic-seeming Matthew Smith (he looked like a gunfighter out of an old western dressed all in black as he was), Lilly had been waiting there to meet them. It was then for the first time that Rose realized that the handsome, tall young man named Wisdom, who'd helped in off-loading the weapons brought in on Myra's aircraft and reloading them aboard the truck, was really Lilly's son. In the next instant, Rose realized that Lilly and Matthew Smith were a thing, the way Lilly just went into Smith's arms like she belonged there.

Myra didn't accompany them; flew her aircraft to a safer

location instead. So Rose Shepherd wound up as the only other woman.

After a round of hugs from Luther and Bill and handshakes with Bob Twobears (Lilly's brother, who just happened to have the same last name as Lilly's ex-husband) and warming up by the fire with a drink, Rose just sort of naturally volunteered to help Lilly with the massive dinner she was making.

Biological destiny? If it were, she'd resigned herself to it. While the men did the important stuff—talked—the women did the inconsequential stuff—cooked. But the funny thing was that it was a lot harder to take a bunch of miscellaneous ingredients and turn them into palatable food than it was to talk and smoke and drink and smoke and talk some more.

As Rose chopped vegetables, Lilly stopped what she was doing, stared at her. "Would you feel a little more comfortable with a change of clothes?"

"All I brought really is more of the same," and Rose gestured to her black T-shirt, black BDU pants, and her boots.

"We're about the same size. This stuff'll keep."

Lilly wore a loose-fitting, comfortable-looking khaki skirt, a little red-and-brown plaid shirt, and a sweater draped over her shoulders and tied around her neck. "All right."

So off they went. . . .

Clark Pietrowski asked, "Is there an accurate estimate of the manpower at this fort with the abominable name?"

Smith laughed.

Luther told Clark, "About six hundred men is the best we've got."

"And we'll have a lot of help from the local tribes," Bill Runningdeer added, "so that'll even the odds a little."

"In the final analysis, this is a desperate plan, but so audacious that it might have a slim chance of being efficacious," Smith said slowly.

Randy Blumenthal, the youngest of them except for Wisdom Twobears (and Blumenthal and the boy seemed to have hit it off instantly), cleared his throat, asked, "How many of us can we get into the compound?"

Holden made an instant decision. "If Smith has no objections, I know he's been talking about you, Wisdom, being in on this, hitting one of the antiaircraft installations we need to knock out. Randy—you're an experienced man, and if you'd have no problems with Wisdom buddying up with you, that'd work well."

Randy Blumenthal looked at the boy, who sat beside him. "No problems."

Holden nodded. "Good, but to answer your question more fully, I'd estimate we can get between one hundred and one hundred twenty-five persons inside. At the best, we'll be outnumbered four to one. But we'll have the element of surprise. Once we've released the prisoners being held there, we should cut those odds in half or better, considering that a good fifty percent of the prisoners probably won't be strong enough to fight.

"Then," David Holden went on, "we'll have a sizable force located outside the fort that can ambush any pursuers coming after us. They won't get them all, but we're not counting on that. What I am counting on is that once the fort's main gates are opened for the pursuit personnel to go after us, the force we'll have waiting outside can penetrate the fort and take it. If we account for seventy-five to a hundred casualties among the PSF personnel, and they dispatch another hundred to two hundred personnel after us, we could cut the garrison strength by fifty percent. So Bob and his Native American force—and Bill, I think you'd be the perfect liaison for that, if that's okay?"

Runningdeer seemed to consider for a moment, then nodded.

Holden picked up his train of thought. "Anyway, Bob and Bill can lead the Native American force against the fort, get anything useful out of the place, and destroy the structure. That way, the fort is out of the picture in the future, and if those of us aboard the train are able to make it through, or even if we aren't, the PSF personnel pursuing us will have nowhere to go to ground and nowhere to resupply."

Holden looked at Bob Twobears, said, "Make certain that any people with farms or ranches or homes in the area take whatever steps they can to protect themselves because the surviving PSF will be desperate for supplies and will likely hit any homestead they come across."

"My people will be ready, and so will the whites."

Holden nodded as Luther Steel said, "The important thing in all of this is to get as many of those military officers as possible free, get them to a place of safety, restore them to health, equip them with travel documents, get them back to where they can do the most good so they can turn their old units around away from the PSF and over onto the side of the Constitution, away from Makowski."

"And let us not forget the dishonorable Mr. Makowski," Smith intoned. "If he is a visitor at the installation that bears his name, and the same goes for Hobart Townes, we ought to do whatever is practical in order to apprehend or, if needed, kill them."

"I'm glad you said that," Holden told Smith. "The optimum thing would be to kidnap Makowski and Townes, use them as bargaining chips with the FLNA and PSF, but the second-best alternative is just to kill them. Regrettable, certainly, as is any death, but if necessary, we must."

And Holden watched young Wisdom Twobears' eyes; they never blinked. . . .

"The task that lay before the Patriots and their Native American allies was great, and their objective fraught with peril," he told the people assembled there on the Hill and across the Mall. And his eyes caught sight of the statue again. "I realized then that I was watching history unfold before my eyes, that if we failed, this nation as we had known it and hoped it to be again would be lost; if we succeeded, what was about to transpire would become the stuff of legend."

Wisdom Twobears looked into the eyes of his wife, then those of his mother, and lastly into the eyes of Matthew Smith, the man who was the only father he had ever known. . . .

Wisdom Twobears watched Matthew Smith fill Araby's feedbag. Matthew had fed the big gray—Wisdom's horse—first, then the other horses in the smallish barn, then, finally, Araby.

As Wisdom forked new hay into one of the stalls, he asked Matthew, "Why is it that you always feed Araby last?"

Matthew looked a little startled by the question, thumbed his black cowboy hat off his forehead, and turned to face him. "Why do you think I feed Araby last?"

"Well, I know with you there has to be a reason."

"Thank you. But what is my reason, then?"

Wisdom thought, finally shrugged his shoulders, telling Matthew, "Beats me."

Matthew laughed. "It's a very simple reason. Since we've moved up here to the cabin, at times we had some shortages, haven't we?"

"Yeah, we sure have."

"Coffee, leather for repairing tack, everything in between. My reasoning is this: Araby is the strongest and fastest horse here; your mount is nearly as strong, nearly as fast, however. And I outweigh you by quite a few pounds. So with you on the back of your horse, your horse will go farther faster than Araby will with me riding her. Araby is part Arabian, of course. The Arab horses have a long history of enduring hardship when necessary. So I feed your animal first. That way, I always know that the best horse and rider combination will always be in top form, and the horse most able to endure a less-than-full belly will be the only animal that might have to make do. Understand? Simple logic. You're nearly my height. If I weighed 148 pounds like you do, I'd feed Araby first. Do you see my reasoning?"

Wisdom Twobears nodded, went back to forking hay. . . .

Rosie was carrying the roast venison. But Holden's eyes, despite the fact he was rather hungry from the exertions of unloading and loading cargo in the snow earlier that evening and having nothing more for lunch than an apple and a peanut-butter sandwich, wasn't that concerned about the food.

Rosie looked beautiful.

Her hair—he'd noticed it getting longer lately—was caught up at the nape of her neck with a bow. She wore a simple white blouse, a gray cardigan sweater over it, and a long, full gray skirt made of corduroy.

There was a certain glow about her that he hadn't remembered seeing before.

She set down the venison, gave him a smile with her pretty gray-green eyes, returned to the kitchen.

Everything on the table smelled unbelievably good, and

all of the meat was wild game—the venison, prairie chicken, rabbit. The bread was fresh from the oven, and on the kitchen counter was a cake and a pie.

Bob Twobears was enthusing, "My sister's a terrific cook. Looks like your friend isn't bad, either."

"No, she's a good cook," Holden agreed, still watching Rosie.

The door opened from the outside, and Holden reached for the Beretta in his trouser band, but it was only Matthew Smith and young Wisdom, back from feeding the horses.

A fire crackled in the hearth.

Rosie came in with a plate of wild rice, set it on the table, then, as Holden stood, helping her with her chair, sat down beside him.

Smith and Wisdom reappeared, hair combed, presumably washed up after their work in the barn.

Smith took the seat at the head of the table.

Lilly sat at the other end of the longish table opposite him.

Wisdom sat down across from Rosie.

Matthew Smith said, "Wisdom, would you say a blessing?"

The boy nodded, saying, "Oh Lord, who gave us minds with which to think and hands with which to turn abstraction into reality and a world of infinite beauty to at once exploit and to protect, bless this food and those who are about to eat it. Forever aid us in the acquisition of knowledge by which we can ever better express our humanity and search for the meaning of your Divinity. Amen."

Holden raised his eyes, looked at the boy, looked at the boy's mother, looked at Smith. Holden pondered the authorship of the prayer, mentally assigned it to Matthew Smith.

Rosie squeezed his hand beneath the table. Holden held her hand tightly.

And David Holden thought of his dead son, the promise always there in his son's eyes, of a future filled with hope and honor and promise.

Holden looked at young Wisdom, then said, "Amen."

CHAPTER NINETEEN

"**Y**ou pull these two pins from here, then place them in the receptacle in the buttstock, here, so you don't lose them, then just pull back on the buttstock, and you have access to the action," Smith was telling the twelve men from Bob Twobears' tribe who sat around him on a mat of overlapping blankets on the cavern floor.

Each of the men took his G-3 and duplicated what Smith had just done. . . .

Rose Shepherd took the Beretta 92F in her hands, telling the men around her, "The large capacity magazines of pistols like the Beretta, the SIG-Sauer, the Smith & Wesson autos, the Taurus, the Glock I carry along with my .45 sometimes, they have a tendency with some shooters to make them get into what we call 'spray and pray' when they shoot. Well, if you've got truckloads of ammo coming up behind you for resupply, that's okay, I guess. But we won't. If you have to use your handgun, use it only at close quarters on this mission, and tell yourself you can only fire two shots without having to reload. Of course, you can fire two shots eight times before having to reload with one of these, but if you tell yourself that you'll waste a lot of ammunition. And these guns are quite capable of good accuracy."

She raised the pistol in a two-hand hold, a point shoulder position, leveled it on the hand-drawn silhouette target.

There was a backstop of hay with stacks of firewood behind it to absorb any bullets and minimize the chance of ricochet, but she was still uncomfortable firing in a cave. "Hearing protectors on!" She hadn't brought tampons (no longer a problem for a while), but had borrowed one from Lilly, tearing chunks of the absorbent material inside to use as plugs.

The twelve men with her either wore shooters' muffs, earplugs, or bits of cloth. Rosie fired, snapping off two shots into the head of the silhouette, the noise echoing and re-echoing in the confines of the cavern.

"But that was a long shot. Stay at the line and watch." Rose used the Beretta's thumb safety like a hammer drop, swiped it back up, halved the distance to the target, now about twelve and a half feet away. From the chest, the first shot double action again, she put two holes about two inches apart into the upper chest and thorax of the silhouette.

Then she lowered the hammer again, upped the safety again, held the gun by her hip. "At really close quarters, regardless of what some combat shooting theories preach, I've always found that getting the gun up so you can see the sights can take too much time. So you line up the body and do this." She fired a double tap, then another and another, then another and another, then brought the pistol up to a point shoulder position and put the last two shots where the silhouette's nose would have been if it had had a real face.

The ten shots she'd fired from the hip in double taps had all but ripped through the abdomen and chest of the silhouette, the last two shots even tighter than the previous aimed shots.

She had always been a good shot, ever since her father, a cop like she had been, had first put a gun in her hand at the age of seven.

He'd had to help her hold it.

But she'd hit what she'd aimed at, after a fashion.

Yet she always hated shooting in front of people because it made her nervous, and if she thought about the people watching her too much and not enough about what she was doing, her marksmanship suffered.

She turned around and looked at the twelve Indians, Sioux, Cheyenne, and at least two other tribes, the names of which she didn't remember. "Just don't forget this. You're not shooting for the tightest group in the world, just to do what you have to do," Rose told them. . . .

"All right, now, come at me." Holden dropped into a crouch, the Defender knife sheathed.

The young Sioux, a dark-haired man of about twenty, a Bowie knife sheathed in his right hand, charged.

Holden sidestepped, tripped the boy, rolled down, pinning the knife hand wrist as gently as he could under his left knee and put the sheathed Defender knife to the man's throat. "Remember what I said about not charging in like something out of a low-budget movie, Irving?"

"Yes, sir." The man nodded. . . .

Bill Runningdeer racked the bolt of the Heckler & Koch submachine gun. "The trick is," he told the dozen men around in a semicircle behind him, "not to fire out the whole magazine every time you pull the trigger. I'm not even going to demonstrate that for you. What you want is a nice, controlled burst. Now, with these H & K MP-5s, that's easy, and that's because of the burst selector position. There's semiauto, which means one shot at a time; full-auto, which means the really experienced man can control his bursts, long or short, at will, just with his finger and the trigger; or this position. Not all of these have this feature, but on these we do. A ratcheting device built into the trigger group itself retains the sear until the number of rounds set has been fired, at which time the sear engages the hammer. This is set for three. Hearing protectors on, please."

Runningdeer fired in burst mode, tearing a small hole into the chest of the homemade silhouette target. . . .

Holden and Smith stood at the center of a circle, surrounded by more than thirty of the Native American volunteers, representing several tribes. "Time was," Smith said, "that every Indian boy grew up knowing how to wrestle for fun, and a lot still do. And obviously, as grown men, we all know how to fight. But what happens under specific danger situations, gentlemen? That's what we're covering. Watch this."

David Holden approached, saying, "Please note, gentlemen, this pistol is unloaded. In real life, you won't be that lucky." Holden worked the slide of the magazineless pistol several times to illustrate. He brought the gun to waist level, stopped before Smith. Smith raised his hands. Holden smiled, under his breath saying, "Don't break my wrist."

Smith's left arm swept down as he sidestepped, swatting the pistol away, Holden backstepping to avoid the knee coming for his crotch and the right hand going to crush his larynx.

"Now, gentlemen," Smith announced. "Who wants to volunteer to try that?"

About half the men raised their hands, the rest tentatively following suit. . . .

Luther Steel told the man opposite him, "Now, come at me and give it all you've got." The man lunged forward, Steel blocking the swinging right, stepping in, stopping just short of his elbow impacting the base of the man's nose. Steel stepped back, told the volunteer, "Thanks."

As the man reseated himself on the blankets with the others, Steel told the men, "We're taught hand-to-hand techniques in the FBI, of course, but none of it is aimed at killing. Unfortunately, times have changed. That's a little trick I picked up from a gentleman named Rocky Saddler. He's old enough to be my father, old enough to have grandfathered some of you. And he could lay out all of us jointly or separately if he had to.

"Strength isn't it," Steel went on, "although it can help, and in Rocky's case, he's quite strong for a man his age or any age. But more important than strength is knowing the right techniques. The elbow is the hardest bone in the human body, as we all know, and with the hardest parts of our body as we attack the softest parts of an opponent's body, we are capable of inflicting the greatest damage.

"So that's something to remember. Take the hardest thing you can pick up and maneuver, and if bare-handed, use the most hardened parts of your body—just above the forehead, for example, once you've learned the technique—and attack the softest, most vulnerable parts of your opponent.

"The nose is an exception. It's bone, so we might think it's hard. Of course bone is hard, but here again we have to consider making our opponent's body work to his disadvantage. When you break the nose properly, you can drive it up through the sinuses and toward the brain, breaking the ethmoid bone. That bone, once penetration is accomplished, will puncture the brain and kill instantly. Regardless of strength, if you know what you're doing, you can kill an opponent who is vastly superior in the physical sense."

Luther Steel hated teaching people how to kill; it went against the grain like nothing else did because all his adult life he had attempted to enforce the law in the least violent manner possible, respecting life.

"Remember," he told them, his voice lowering, "we have

no facility for taking prisoners or maintaining them. Every one of the Presidential Strike Force we kill on the day of the raid will be one less to come after us, raid a private home, threaten unarmed women and children, or be around for the next battle. That's the way it is, unfortunately. We can comfort ourselves with the knowledge that we didn't start this, and perhaps that will help us to be strong.

"Now, remember, hard to soft. Let's have a volunteer!"

Hands raised. . . .

By the time they'd gotten to bed, they'd only cuddled, held each other, slept.

She had wanted more.

As they rode their horses back toward the cabin at Trapper Springs, she watched David.

He didn't look perfectly at home on horseback, but he was in control.

He was in control of her too, now, and she had to tell him.

Maybe tonight.

CHAPTER TWENTY

*T*here were fresh welts on Emma's back when Kearney undressed her.

But he knew they were watching.

"You don't wanna have sex with me, do you, but then you do?"

He didn't quite understand her. "You're very beautiful."

"You still love her, your girl, don't you?"

Linda Effingham. Kearney closed his eyes, opened them again quickly. "Yes, but you're helping me to handle it." The last part was a lie because having another woman now only made it worse for him, only made him feel Linda's death still more. "We can help each other," Kearney told Emma at last.

Her blue eyes held the promise of a smile. He touched his lips to hers, and she pressed herself against him, her nipples hot and tight against his chest.

As he touched her, kissed her, held her, he was very aware of Montenegro and Borsoi watching him. Borsoi was a type Kearney had often encountered professionally, extremely competent, impersonal, and, when necessary, totally detached. Under other circumstances, Kearney couldn't see himself having taken to Borsoi as a friend, but at least the man had some merits, however dubious.

Montenegro, on the other hand, was a piece of garbage,

the sort of soul one found floating along in a rain gutter out of an alley.

It was Montenegro who beat Emma with a belt; it was, doubtless, Montenegro whose idea it had been to kill Linda. It was Montenegro who sat smiling now, perhaps masturbating, watching this on video.

And Geoffrey Kearney had no choice but to give the man a good show.

"Come here to me," he told the girl, taking her into his arms, carrying her to the bed, setting her down, then starting out of his pants.

CHAPTER TWENTY-ONE

*T*hey'd made love three nights out of the last six, and each time, she hadn't told David.

The Indians were naturals at picking up what they were being taught, already for the most part at least modestly skilled with firearms—from hunting, for example—and many of them natural athletes.

The older men who could not be expected to do the intensely physical things would be part of the force lying in wait outside the fort, ready to enter it as the train left and (hopefully) David and the rest made good their escape.

The younger ones, the ones who took best to the accelerated training, they would be the ones who entered under the false floors that were already being prepared for use in the boxcars. Today, she worked again with the three dozen women who would be assisting in the attacks on the antiaircraft facilities.

They were good, and what they lacked in skills brought to the instruction they made up in enthusiasm.

And it was perhaps because of the women, she realized, that she had not yet told David she carried their child.

What if he did with her what he had done with Bill Runningdeer, assigned her to hitting the antiaircraft facilities, just because it was a safer job, and if something went wrong, there was at least the possibility for escape.

What if he wouldn't let her fight at all?

The concept of a man letting her or not letting her do something was somewhat alien to her, at least ever since the death of her father.

Sure, she'd worked for male watch commanders and all the other male police brass all her adult life, but she could always tell them to take a hike or something worse, even if it meant her job.

But with David she genuinely wanted to do as he wanted her to do.

The feeling was at once comforting and frightening.

But whatever he told her, she would be on that train, be with him when he needed her.

She realized Lilly was staring at her.

Rose set down her coffee cup.

"What's bothering you?"

"I don't understand," Rose said.

Lilly smiled, lowered her voice, even though the men were still at the caverns, except for Wisdom, who had accompanied her home and was now outside feeding and caring for his horse. She should have stayed at the caverns. Lilly said, "You're having Professor Holden's baby, aren't you?"

Rose Shepherd was happy she'd set down the coffee. For a second, she didn't answer, then, "How'd you know?"

"Your eyes. A man wouldn't know, but another woman can tell. You can't be very far along."

Rose shook her head. "I'm not. And if David finds out, he's going to want to—"

"Leave you someplace safe? And what's wrong with that?"

"Everything!"

"No. What is wrong with safeguarding your unborn child? If something should happen—"

"If David died, I'd die. It's that simple and damn

straight," Rose told her. She had been avoiding cigarettes, for the health of the baby, but this would be her third one of the day and the day was almost gone, and she wanted to cry and her hands were shaking.

She lit a cigarette.

"I assume he knows how much you love him?"

Rose bit her lower lip, lit up, nodded, shrugged. "Yeah," she said through a mouthful of smoke.

"So then, the only reason you're afraid to tell him about the baby is because you're afraid he'll leave you behind this time. Right?"

"Yeah." Rose nodded. "So?"

"Do you think he wants the baby?"

Rose had thought about that a lot, and every time she did, she inevitably, no matter how circuitous the thought process, came to the same conclusion: David wanted the child. "Yeah." She was beginning to sound like a broken record.

"Then don't you think he'll be angry that you have this sensational information for him, something that will give new meaning and hope to his life, and you're just withholding it from him?"

"I'm not being selfish, I'm—"

"There's nothing wrong with selfishness, Rosie. Think about how terrific you'll feel when he takes you into his arms, asks you every question he can think of about the baby, about you, just everything like that! You'll feel so terrific, so special. How do you think I felt with Wisdom inside me? And my husband was an alcoholic bum. I hadn't met Matthew yet. You're lucky. You've met the man of your dreams already. Tell him. If he orders you to stay out of the fighting, worry about that when it happens. Don't ruin now."

Rose walked over to her, put her arms around her, leaned

her head down against Lilly Twobears' shoulder. "Thank you."

Behind her, she heard the door open from the outside, the moaning of the wind, the sound of men's voices.

One of them was David's voice. . . .

The bedroom they shared was the young boy's bedroom, but the bed was full sized and, by far, beat sleeping on ground clothes and an air mattress as they did in the camp outside Metro.

David Holden was more than slightly worried. There should have been a radio contact with Mitch Diamond, but there wasn't. In fact, Mitch was three days' overdue.

But there was nothing to be done about it except try again at the appointed times and hope for the best.

Rosie lay in Holden's arms.

The air in the bedroom was a little cool, the wind outside high and cold. But beneath the blankets and the quilt, in the flannel sheets, they were warm.

Naked, Rosie molded her body against his.

There was something in their lovemaking that he recognized, tried to avoid thinking about. It was desperation.

Take the moment, live it, enjoy it, savor it, because it might be the last.

Her hands touched him. Holden touched his lips to her left breast.

"Let me on top for a little," Rosie told him.

Holden rolled onto his back, Rosie getting on top of him, her fingers moving in the hair on his chest.

And then her right hand left his chest, touched at his organ, and suddenly he was inside her.

"David?"

Her body moved on him. He raised up on his elbows, his

hands at her breasts, her mouth coming down to his. He kissed her hard.

"David?"

Holden leaned back, breathing, feeling himself in her. "What?"

"I'm having a baby, our baby."

He slipped out of her. "What?"

She still straddled him, her fingers touching at his face. "I'm pregnant; we're pregnant, David."

"Uhh—" He started to say something, started to think of lots of things.

Instead, he pushed her over beside him, onto her back, then came between her legs. "I love you, Rosie," Holden told her, entered her.

"Are you—"

"Happy?" Holden's mouth came down over hers. Her body moved under him. "Yes, I'm happy—I want this baby so much," David Holden told her.

He had realized that someday this would happen. He hadn't known quite what he would say.

How he would feel.

But he wanted Rosie, wanted their baby. He arched her back with his hands, her legs wrapping around him.

Her body shook. So did his.

And after a while, he sank into her arms, touched her lips with his. And he realized that his right hand rested against her abdomen, and he kissed her mouth.

CHAPTER TWENTY-TWO

"**N**o, dammit!"

"Why not?"

Holden took one of her cigarettes, took her lighter, lit the cigarette, exhaled as he said, "Because you could get hurt, or even killed, and the baby too! That's why! And what the hell are you doing with cigarettes when you're pregnant?"

He inhaled, exhaled.

"I am going, David Holden! I love you. I am carrying your child. I wish to God everyday we were married. But I am going with you, David."

"You could get—"

"So what? If I'm not with you, I'm dead anyway, dammit! Think about it. For just a damn minute, think about! Please! I want to be with you."

Holden's throat felt tight. His hands were shaking. He inhaled, but didn't get that much smoke into his lungs. He stubbed out her cigarette. "You, uhh—I—I love you, and if you died, or—"

"David? Please?" She reached out toward him with both hands, and there were tears in her eyes.

He looked at her hard. She wore one of her black T-shirts, nothing else, not even panties.

Holden sat back down on the bed. "If you died, Rosie, what the hell would I have to—" He looked away.

"David? If one of us died, I mean, I—" She fell on her

knees at his feet, her lips touching at his bare thigh, her arms hugging his leg. "Just hold me, please?"

David Holden drew her head against him, held her there.

Her lips touched at his abdomen. Her arms still hugged his leg. If he lost Rosie, he lost everything.

And man can't lose everything twice and live, Holden told himself.

And he looked at her. He kissed her hair. He buried his face in her hair.

She was his lover. She was as much wife to him as if a thousand priests had said words over them, more. But she was his friend.

"Can't you—"

"Why should I? Isn't it my fight, too, David? Tell me what to do, please?"

He wanted to tell her, as he had told her, that she couldn't go.

Lover. Friend. Respect.

David Holden drew Rosie Shepherd up from her knees, onto his lap, her arms going around his neck, her head burrowing into his shoulder, her legs drawing up so her knees were almost touching her chin. "Tell me what to do, David?"

David Holden rocked her in his arms.

He realized there were tears in his eyes too, and he tried to sniff them back, couldn't, let them come, held her, felt her body trembling against his. When you were born, they should give you a manual, tell you what to do, how to react, what to say. And then he realized they did, or He did.

The manual was conscience, and its dictums were acted upon by the heart.

He held her tight, fought back the tears, tried to make his voice sound right when he said to her, "We stay together, all the time. If it happens, then it happens to both of us. And if it doesn't, then we get out together. But I can't lose you. Or the baby."

"I know," Rosie sobbed, her head against his face, her lips pouting out, touching at his cheek, the salty taste of tears in her kiss. "What good would it be, David?"

She was right, Holden realized.

There could be no good in anything.

He held her.

Holden closed his eyes. He saw Elizabeth and Dave and Meg and little Irene. His perfect family. He saw their faces dead, no life, no happiness, nothing.

If he died, and there was heaven or the other place, what would he tell Elizabeth? "I still love you, but I love Rosie too." Tell her that?

He held Rosie so tight that he was afraid for a moment he would crush the breath from her. She was crying hard now. So was he. And David Holden realized something. If there was someplace after this, Elizabeth would understand. No longer fighting the tears, he whispered hoarsely against Rosie's hair, "My wife, Elizabeth, she would have liked you. And Dave and Meg and Irene would have loved you. All four of them, they would have figured you were just the best person, Rosie."

They would attack the fort on the morning after tomorrow, unless it was already tomorrow. And this night coming would be when the antiaircraft installations would be hit.

"I'm going to ask Matthew and Lilly if they know a minister or a priest or somebody. We don't need him, but I'd like to do it," Holden whispered, held her.

Rosie just cried.

CHAPTER TWENTY-THREE

He was a short man, balding, had a southern accent you could cut with a knife, Rose thought, but none of the southern speech patterns.

And he had a nice smile.

She was wearing the best thing in Lilly's closet. Lilly had insisted. It was a traditional Indian woman's wedding dress, made of bleached white soft sueded buckskin, with beadwork on the bodice, in the skirt, and fringe everywhere. For a little while, when she'd first pulled it on over her head, she'd felt foolish.

But it was a wedding dress.

Clark gave her away, and she hadn't even had to ask him more than once.

And David wore a suit, black, with a black knit tie and white shirt, borrowed from Matthew Smith.

Over her head, she wore a shawl that was made of lace.

Rose Shepherd lowered her eyes, held David's arm tight.

Lilly was her maid of honor. Lilly was very beautiful.

"Dearly beloved," the little man in clerical collar, pullover sweater, and gray woolen pants began. "We are gathered here together in the sight of God to join this man and this woman in holy matrimony. . . ." This was the happiest day of her life, Rose Shepherd told herself. Why was she crying?

Luther Steel handed David the ring David had for her.

"I do," she whispered from beneath her veil.

"I do," David said, his voice firm, strong beside her, his right hand folded over both her hands.

"I now pronounce you man and wife, and whomsoever God hath joined together let no man put asunder. You may kiss the bride."

David turned her around, took her in his arms. "Together always, Rosie," David whispered, kissing her so hard Rosie Shepherd—and she thought of herself that way for the thousandth time, the ten thousandth time. She was Rose Holden. Her husband kissed her so hard, she could barely breathe.

CHAPTER TWENTY-FOUR

*T*he rings they each wore were identical except for size. Matthew Smith had made them on the blacksmith's anvil in the barn, hammered them, forged them out of nails.

David Holden looked at the ring on the third finger of his left hand, then pulled on his glove.

He gave the signal to Bill Runningdeer and Luther Steel. While he waited, he looked at the sunset over the white-crusted peaks to the west.

There was the sound of a flare being fired, and in the next instant, there was a small explosion. That would be the satellite dish that handled incoming and outgoing communications between the antiaircraft installation and Fort Makowski.

There was a sound unlike anything he'd ever heard, and Holden looked toward its origin. One of the young Native Americans had let out an Indian war whoop.

Beside him, Rosie whispered, "Here we go."

"Here we go, Mrs. Holden." And side by side, they were up, clambering over the snowbank, running, gunfire starting from the firing holes in the bunker wall, a string of explosions around the structure as Clark Pietrowski and Tom LeFleur detonated the land mines that served as part of the perimeter defense.

An orange wash seemed to bathe the snow in light. Holden squinted against the sun.

Three of the men from the bunker appeared in the open, two of them firing M-16 assault rifles, the third holding a grenade. Holden and Rosie fired their weapons simultaneously, cutting down that third man, the grenade tumbling into the snow, a shortfall, the two men with M-16s running. The grenade detonated.

David Holden shouted, "Follow me!"

They charged along the rise toward the summit. . . .

The first attack behind them now, they split up, Blumenthal and young Wisdom Twobears with a unit of some forty-five Native Americans, most of them armed with lever actions, shotguns, and revolvers, any firearm that could be used against the Presidential Strike Force, armed with some of the most modern military weapons. Holden remembered the media-generated hysteria against modern firearms shortly before the Troubles began, and the unbridled enthusiasm with which the media and some members of Congress had attacked the Second Amendment on every ground possible, attempting to divide and conquer those who believed in the right to keep and bear arms.

And so men were reduced to fighting for freedom with guns that, albeit they were a century behind current technology, were illegally possessed.

Bill Runningdeer took another unit, all Native Americans. LeFleur and Clark Pietrowski took a third.

With the antiaircraft installations possibly on full alert by now, Holden, Rosie, Steel, and Matthew Smith hit the fifth and last of them.

At first, the idea of simultaneous attacks timed to coincide with the assault on Fort Makowski had been decided upon. But then Holden had realized there was the possibility of turning potential disadvantage to advantage.

If, indeed, a trap awaited them at Fort Makowski, the

garrison would already be on full alert. Attacking the anti-aircraft batteries in advance would have to provoke a response from the fort, siphoning off more of its manpower, hence an advantage—Holden hoped.

It was full darkness now, and the cold was numbing. David and Rosie Holden moved at the head of two dozen poorly armed but dedicated men and women, toward the summit atop which was set the last of the bunkers.

David Holden spoke into his radio, "Advance element, this is Strike Team Leader, come in. Over."

Steel's voice came back, crystal clear and without static. "This is Advance Element. Reading you loud and clear. Some activity here. They're expecting us. Surprises are ready. Over."

Holden looked at the black-faced Rolex on his left wrist. The sweep second hand was approaching the inverted triangle at the twelve position. "Watch for my signal, Advance Element. Strike Team Leader out."

Rosie wisely had brought along two Heckler & Koch flare pistols from among the store of arms and equipment taken from the underground Delta facility; and now Holden turned to the eighteen-year-old Sioux behind him, saying, "Rod, fire the flare on my signal."

"Right, Professor."

Rosie gave the magazine in her G-3 a whack.

Holden did a last-minute equipment check, one eye on his watch.

He told the young Indian, "All right, fire the starburst."

Rod Whitecloud fired the flare. Holden shouted, "Follow me!"

From the opposite side of the installation, explosions began in a ripple effect. It was the Hawk MM-1 grenade launcher. There was a louder explosion still, one of the few and precious LAW rockets fired from Holden's unit, directly at the reinforced door into the bunker. Holden, his wife, Rosie, beside him, and the men and women of the Native American force around them, ran toward the bunker.

Two sentries opened fire with M-16s. Rosie fired her G-3, two short bursts, bringing one of the men down. At Holden's left, just as he was about to fire on the other PSF man, one of the Indian women brought a lever-action .30-30 to her shoulder and fired, with a single shot bringing the man down.

Holden started to laugh, kept running. They were nearing the main entrance to the bunker. . . .

Matthew Smith, two Arapaho men and a woman from the Cheyenne with him, reached the top of the bunker. His semiautomatic H & K rifle was slung behind him. The three Indians were armed with revolvers of various persuasions— one of them was an old Colt single action that in years gone by would have fetched a handsome price on the collector market—and bolt-action rifles in deer calibers.

There was a firing port for the antiaircraft gun located there, as well as two smaller firing ports for remote-controlled machine guns that were part of the facility's defense system.

Both of the smaller firing ports were opening.

Smith warned the three people with him. "Watch out!" As he said it, he pulled a high explosive grenade from the pocket of his sheepskin coat and tore the cotter pin free, then lobbed it into the open firing port.

Smith threw himself down onto the dome of the structure, prone beside the three people with him. The dome trembled as the explosion came, and Smith felt pieces of concrete from the dome itself and perhaps bits and pieces of the machine gun falling on him, heard them falling around him despite the ringing in his ears from the concussion.

He was up, running, reaching the gaping four-foot wound in the dome that moments earlier had been a neatly finished eighteen-inch square opening. Smith lobbed a second grenade through the opening, ran back, dropped prone again.

The explosion, well below him inside the base of the dome, was barely audible this time. But as soon as it came and went, he was up again, the three Native Americans with him.

Coiled cross body on the woman's torso was a fifty-foot length of rope, knotted at eighteen-inch intervals. She shrugged out of the rope and tossed the weighted end over into the hole.

Smith screwed his black Stetson tighter to his head, grabbed the rope, and let himself over into the hole, then started down.

His cowboy-booted feet wrapped around one of the knots as he peered below him into the smoke. Smith coughed, snarled under his breath, lowered himself into he knew not what.

From the drag in the rope below him and his gauging of the distance he'd traveled, he realized he was near the bottom. At the moment the thought crossed Smith's mind, gunfire tore into the rope, just above his head, and Smith jumped, hitting the floor harder than he wanted to, buckling his knees, going into a sideways roll, his left shoulder slamming into something hard, his back feeling every millimeter in the surface of his rifle. But through the smoke, he couldn't see the object he'd hit.

Gunfire slammed into the object, whatever it was, and Smith's right hand flashed to the full-flap El Paso rig at his right hip, tearing the Beretta free, his right thumb offing the safety as his first finger snapped against the trigger, a single shot, then another and another and another.

But as he fired, he was moving, another burst of gunfire as

some of the smoke cleared. Smith fired toward the figure he saw with an M-16, cutting the man down.

There was no time to grab the dead man's weapon, nor to grab for the HK-91 slung across his back.

There was a doorway, and Smith heard shouting from the other side, stepped back, a man coming through just as Smith pulled away. Smith's right hand, still holding the Beretta 92F, crashed downward at the base of the man's skull, putting him down.

A second man stepped through the doorway, and Smith fired at him point-blank, putting a bullet through his thorax.

Smith shifted the Beretta to his left hand, swung the HK-91 forward, rotated the safety to fire.

Smith dropped the Beretta's thumb safety, the hammer dropping just as it should. He stabbed the pistol into his gunbelt so both hands were free for the rifle.

He started through the doorway. . . .

David Holden and Rosie reached the blown-out doorway into the bunker, Holden pulling back, spraying his G-3 through the opening, up and down, side to side.

He shifted magazines, gave the signal, Rosie coming in from the right, Holden from the left, the Native American fighters behind them.

Beyond the doorway was a smooth-walled corridor. Smoke was everywhere. A moment earlier, he'd heard the sounds of explosions from the dome-shaped roof. Smith was on schedule.

There was an explosion from the far side of the building.

That would be Luther Steel with the bulk of the remaining force, coming in through the bunker's emergency exit.

Holden broke into a run, hugging the wall, Rosie opposite him doing the same.

Holden stepped up onto it, edged forward.

Rosie was still opposite him.

From the smoky interior beyond, Holden heard a voice, Smith's voice. "Hold your fire. Everyone in here's dead except us."

David Holden shouted back, "Code word, Smith."

"A rather silly code word, but you realize that." The purpose of the code word was to guard against an enemy forcing one element or another to lure other members of the force into a trap. And now Smith gave it. "Cha-cha."

Rosie smiled. "Did you like the cha-cha?"

Holden just shook his head, started through the doorway.

CHAPTER TWENTY-FIVE

*P*atrols of Presidential Strike Force personnel were everywhere in the mountains and the valleys between them, and as the Patriots horsebacked along a ridge toward the rendezvous with the force that would be used in the morning's raid on Fort Makowski, several times it was necessary to stop, keep their animals as totally silent as possible, wait for as long as twenty minutes, but most times less, until the patrol below them well below the ridge line had passed.

Then remount, on again.

Rose Holden—it was fun thinking of herself like that— now appreciated a phrase she'd always heard in westerns: saddle sore.

Her butt hurt.

They kept on riding, the moon bright above them, clouds scudding past it at frenetic speed on a wind that cut through her M-65 jacket, the liner, the woolen sweater under it, and what she wore under that. She covered her legs and lower body with her rain poncho, using it as a way of cheating the wind. But even the poncho was stiff with the cold.

They rode on.

At least her horse was nice, she thought, didn't try throwing her, didn't try turning its head around to nip at her, had what she considered an easy gait. The longer she rode, the more she got the rhythm of it.

She told herself she could get to like this, but only someplace where it was warm. Why weren't they riding along some beach somewhere with the surf lapping around them, just she and David?

In a gust of wind, snow blew off a flat rock her horse passed and bathed her face in its icy spray.

Reality.

She was cold, tired, wanted to be in bed with her new husband and realized that in another few hours both she and David would be risking their lives.

Sometimes, Rose thought, life sucked.

CHAPTER TWENTY-SIX

Alone, Geoffrey Kearney lay in bed. Awake, he stared at the ceiling.

After Emma left, he'd been unable to sleep.

Linda.

And his thoughts of revenge.

He'd been given the date for his speech on live national television, on all the major networks.

Tomorrow.

Or was it today already.

He glanced at his watch.

Today.

Kearney ran the plan through his mind once again. If he were extremely skillful and lucky, he just might make it through this thing alive. But a considerable amount of skill and luck would be necessary, maybe more than he possessed of either.

He had already made it clear that he should be armed in the event of an assassination attempt by the government on the FLNA leader, Vindicator. But beforehand, he'd known that one of the conditions of the televised speech and the question and answer session was that FLNA personnel, much like Third World leaders had often been when appearing before the United Nations, could be armed, a sort of temporary diplomatic immunity from the laws that disarmed American citizens.

Clearly, the murder of Borsoi and Montenegro would be the easiest (not to mention most satisfying) part. He had to get off the stage, out of the building, and away by car. And that too he had planned for.

But there, the luck entered in.

He was counting on hysteria, but a controlled hysteria. What would the U.S. officials do, after all, when he assassinated the FLNA leaders? If he pulled the trigger on one of the newsmen assigned to ask him the prepared questions, on the other hand, he knew the reaction.

The trick was, he knew, to combine the two predictable reactions to serve his own best interests.

The most important of the newspeople who would be questioning him would be network anchor Colin Best. Best was often spoken of as a possible candidate for public office in the future, was the liberal darling, was the most important commodity his network possessed, and was courted by the other networks with promised ridiculous sums of money to leave his current post and come to work for one or the other of them.

Colin Best was, clearly, valuable.

Reduced to its most basic terms, the success or failure of his plan rested squarely on the carefully tailored shoulders of Colin Best.

Geoffrey Kearney closed his eyes, but opened them again. He saw Linda Effingham when he closed his eyes.

He started reciting his schedule for tomorrow, like another man might count sheep. Up at eight, then a good run, a little harder and longer than usual, then a swim, then the perfunctory and, by then, quite necessary ablutions. Then rehearsal with Borsoi and Montenegro, then a light lunch, then dress for the occasion—they had some sort of camouflage outfit for him that had been meticulously tailored for a properly rakish fit. Then off to the site of the televised speech. Sound and light checks, then a light snack of some high-energy food. Makeup (he told himself he could get through that) and just at seven P.M. eastern daylight time, on stage. "Live! From Metro!" Kearney caught himself smiling.

He tried closing his eyes again. With all that skill and luck, if he had it, he'd be alive to smile again.

CHAPTER TWENTY-SEVEN

*T*he last of the jigsaw pieces for the artificial floors were being loaded aboard the trucks, to fit together something like a Chinese puzzle box, Holden mused—he hoped. If boxcars different from standard would be used this day, the whole thing would be lost.

Holden tried not to think about that.

Rosie was away on her own, changing, the only woman who would be among the force that was to enter Fort Makowski (and hopefully, leave alive). He still wrestled with his conscience over his decision to let her come along, terrified that she or the baby, would somehow be injured, even killed.

But there was no choice. He respected her too much to deny her.

He dressed in the back of one of the trucks, most of the personnel already "costumed." And the PSF battle dress utilities were just that, a costume. The camouflage pattern was grossly unrealistic, in a genuine warfare situation, where cammies would really be required, just unnatural enough to show up anyone wearing a set as an instant target.

The right boots, the right gunbelt, and the beret, of course, latest addition to PSF standard field dress.

Only the gun and magazines—his own Beretta 92F—were his own. Beneath the BDU blouse, he wore his shoulder holster with the second Beretta, the 92F compact, Crain Defender knife, and two twenty-round magazines.

The field jackets, basic M-65s, were in the same ill-conceived cammie pattern as the BDUs. He pulled his on. The liners were heavier than standard M-65s, something at least to say in their behalf.

The Desert Eagle .44 semiauto, the one he'd inherited from Rufus Burroughs, Holden stuffed into the waistband of his BDUs. The Southwind Sanctions SAS holster he normally carried it in had to stay behind. The spare magazines for the Desert Eagle he stashed in his pockets.

Before donning the beret, he looked in the small, rectangular metal signal mirror that was part of his survival gear. The fake mustache he wore looked real enough and would certainly be within regs for the PSF. And he stared at his face. "Don't lose what you have," David Holden whispered to himself.

Rosie. Their unborn baby.

He returned the mirror to the musette bag with the rest of his gear. He took his wallet from the black BDUs he'd just removed. Inside his wallet was a photograph, laminated, worn around the edges. Elizabeth. Dave, Meg, and little Irene. Holden touched his hand to the photo. And there was another photo, newer, less dog-eared. Rosie. He stared at both photos simultaneously. His family, all of them, forever. He put the wallet inside the musette bag. It could not accompany him.

Holden tucked the beret into his pocket, determined not to put it on until the last minute. If it had meant something honorable, he would have donned it then.

But as the newest symbol of the Presidential Strike Force, it stood only for dishonor and evil.

Holden walked to the back of the truck, threw open the sliding door, jumped out. Steel and Smith were there, attired identically in PSF uniforms. "I feel somewhat less than sartorially resplendent like this." Smith laughed, gesturing over his attire.

"You look 'somewhat less than sartorially resplendent,' Smith," Steel told him. Holden lit a cigarette. Steel, the humor gone from his voice, said, "I think it's almost time, David."

David Holden knew that, inhaled hard on his cigarette.

CHAPTER TWENTY-EIGHT

*R*ose looked at herself in her compact mirror. "Rose Shepherd Holden. Mrs. Rose Shepherd Holden. Mrs. David Holden. Dr. and Mrs. David Holden." She liked that one a lot.

She put the mirror down and began to strip out of her black BDUs and into the hated uniform of the Presidential Strike Force. She not only despised what it stood for, but the camouflage pattern was as tacky looking as a cheap print housedress.

She dressed in it anyway, but left on her black T-shirt over her bra and the white plastic upside-down Ken Null shoulder holster with her little Model 60 Smith in it. The T-shirt's neck was low enough it wouldn't show when the uniform blouse was buttoned.

She removed any vestige of lipstick, nothing else to worry about except the little gold stud earrings she wore. She removed those, put them in her bag. The little holes in her earlobes were irreconcilable. But if somebody got that close and looked suspicious, she'd shoot the person anyway.

Finally, she got to the beret. This was going to be tricky. After several tries, she got her hair stuffed into it. There were women among the PSF, but very few, and the less attention she called to herself the better they'd be. She'd considered cutting her hair to a man's length, but decided that she could get away without it—at least she convinced herself that she could. The hair looked okay, and the same remedy for closeness applied.

Holding the compact mirror at arm's length, she was able to see herself in sufficient detail. And for once, she was glad she was on the flat-chested side. In any event, she wanted to nurse the baby and that would take care of her flat chestedness, but hopefully not too much.

She was a wife now. In about seven and a half months, she'd be a mother.

Scary, a little, but neat. She left the truck, slinging the gas mask bag cross body and securing the strap around her waist. Hopefully, the wind would remain calm when the masks equipped with standard filters would be needed.

CHAPTER TWENTY-NINE

Steinmetz AFB was the kicker, now that it was under direct control of the Presidential Strike Force, Holden knew, but there was no way to compensate for it except with hope that reason and patriotism would prevail over unlawful orders, and the remote chance that, if they were able to successfully snatch de facto President Roman Makowski, threats of killing him might force the Air Force units off.

So he dismissed any thoughts of what could happen if the fighter squadrons at Steinmetz were scrambled and sent after them, relying on his two options there, however slim. David Holden did not want to order Runningdeer and LeFleur and Blumenthal and the two Kalispell Patriots who commanded the total of five antiaircraft installations to open fire on U.S. planes.

In the camouflage-pattern-painted half-track trucks—the pattern was the same as used on the uniforms—they convoyed into the small town of Fort Devon below Widow's Table, where their objective, Fort Makowski, was set.

Fort Devon was like something out of a western painting, two rows of buildings, many of them false fronted, set across from each other over a wide unpaved street. Other buildings formed residential blocks behind the two rows on either side, and at the far end of town, a covered passenger platform and a series of low, peaked roof warehouses stood near several large but empty animal corrals. Bisecting the area bounded by the platform and warehouses and corrals was a complex-looking aggregate of railroad tracks, blind sidings, a carousel-style turnaround, more tracks.

This was the reason for Fort Devon's existence. It served the railroad.

Many of the track sections were still snow covered or, where exposed, rusted from disuse. But two sections were perfectly clear, the rails gleaming in the streaks of sunlight penetrating between the mountains below the gray-blue overcast.

It was sunrise.

These tracks led away from Fort Devon, eventually to Helena, Great Falls, even Spokane on the other side of the upthrusting chimney of Idaho. The other set led up through the mountains and toward the isolated peninsula of rock that was Widow's Table, perched overlooking Fool's Canyon and Hardship River, the river's white-water rapids gouging a cut through the canyon like the slash of a dulling knife, tearing, twisting.

A train was panting in the yard, a spare engine, three fifty-foot-long boxcars, two of the cattle cars of the type used to haul the kidnapped military and naval personnel to the detention center at the fort, a flat car, and a caboose in tow. From over Holden's shoulder, Charlie Thunderclap announced, "That's a GP38-2, sixteen cylinder, blower-aspirated, water-cooled diesel. Best locomotive in the world for these mountains. The one behind it is the same. They're made by General Motors Corporation's Electro-Motive Division. With a 58:18 gear ratio, they crank out eighty-two miles per hour all out." Charlie Thunderclap was one of the Sioux tribesmen, and for the last decade until he returned home to aid his tribe during the Troubles, he had been a railroad engineer over the border in British Columbia, Alberta, and Saskatchewan.

Holden stared at the train through the partially steamed window of the half-track truck's cab.

Around it, men and women from the town of Fort Devon moved, loading cargo into one of the boxcars. Atop the cars, PSF personnel stood guard, M-16 rifles at the ready.

It reminded Holden of things he'd read and archival footage he'd seen of Nazi Germany.

This was what the United States had become.

The boxcars were the type they had planned on.

"Let's go," Holden said.

Smith, beside him at the wheel, picked up the radio microphone. "This is Convoy Leader. Proceed into Fort Devon as planned. Do not acknowledge. Out." The phrase "as planned" meant they were going ahead and would assault the train according to plan. . . .

David Holden wore the rank of colonel, just enough to be certain of outranking anyone he met short of Roman Makowski and Presidential Advisor Hobart Townes, including the commander of Fort Makowski's garrison, Lieutenant Colonel Eugene Lewis Hackler.

In the Navy, Holden's last rank had been commander, close enough.

Holden stepped down from the passenger side of the lead half-track truck, his Defender knife up the left sleeve of his field jacket. Matching the camouflage paint on the trucks had been difficult, but as he looked at the convoy, it was hard to tell the few genuine captured PSF vehicles from the ones painted to look identical to them.

Smith, wearing the rank of master sergeant, took the orders from his breast pocket.

The sole function of the orders—forged for them by a seventy-three-year-old Arapaho woman who had spent her life (when not caring for her family) as an artist—was to buy them a few seconds here. Once the train was captured, the real orders would be taken and used to admit them through the fort's perimeter security.

Holden, Rosie, Smith, Steel, Bob Twobears, and three other Indians left their idling vehicles and approached the train on foot through the snow.

The sun was higher now, which meant it was all but obscured by the blue-gray overcast.

Holden glanced over his shoulder.

Harry Blackdog, one of the Kalispell Patriots and leader of the second element, should be in position in the woods just beyond the town limits, ready to come in should things go wrong at the train.

Holden mentally crossed his fingers that they would not.

They neared the train, walked parallel to it now, seeing men and women inside the two cattle cars huddled together in obvious misery. Holden felt a glow of pride as one of the women tried spitting at them through the bars because of the uniforms they wore, and one of the male officers shouted, "Fuck you!"

They kept walking, only Twobears' three men who were dressed as enlisted personnel carrying M-16s, Holden, Rosie, and the others armed only with pistols.

One of the PSF officers, evidently supervising the boxcar loading, which seemed about half completed, turned toward them, saluted. "Good morning, sir!"

Holden returned the salute. "Lieutenant. What's going on here?" He'd learned that in his own military career, to always put someone on the defensive if it were necessary to distract him.

"Uhh, sir?"

"You heard me, Lieutenant. What the hell is going on here?"

Holden stood about three feet from the young officer now.

"We're loading supplies—fresh food and stuff—for the fort, sir."

"Show him the orders, Sergeant Smith."

"Yes, sir." Matthew Smith handed over the faked orders, then said, "Begging the colonel's pardon, sir, but I just remembered we should take care of the clutch on that half-track."

That was a code sequence that Smith had spotted the obvious key personnel. "Very good, Sergeant. See to it."

"Yes, sir." And now, Smith spoke as if addressing the three noncoms. "The third truck, gentlemen. Look on top of the dashboard to the center for the clipboard. Get the tools you need from the second truck toward the rear. There's a flat container that'll have what you need. Look for it anywhere there." Translation: One man on the third boxcar at the center had the drop on them, then the man at the rear of the second car. Everyone on the flatcar had to be taken out. Smith went on. "I'll take care of getting what we need from the first truck." Smith and Steel, who were to work in tandem, would eliminate the men on the roof of the first boxcar, beside which they stood.

Holden watched as the lieutenant perused the orders. Holden didn't want to give him too much time, snatched them back. "As you can see, we're to relieve Lieutenant Colonel Hackler, and as is obvious from the lack of security here, for very good reasons."

"But, sir, uhh—"

Holden waited for the first shot that would be his signal.

There was a burst of assault rifle fire. Holden snapped his left arm forward and the Defender knife slipped downward into his intentionally gloved hand, the blade sliding across his palm, his left fist closing on the handle, then ramming the knife edge upward into the PSF lieutenant's abdomen, primary edge up, ripping, his right hand going for the full-sized Beretta at his right side. Rosie shot the lieutenant between the eyes.

Out of the left corner of his peripheral vision, he saw Smith, in a half crouch, Smith's Beretta 92F at the end of his outstretched right arm as he fired toward the roof of the first boxcar, Steel's gun in action only a beat slower. Holden fired a double tap into the lieutenant's chest, shooting the body off his knife. Holden wheeled right, pumping two more shots into one of the boxcar guards who was already hit but was firing his M-16. Rosie put two double taps into a guard on the roof of the second car, the man's M-16 spraying downward.

There was a single furrow of bullet holes through the snow about a yard from Holden's feet.

Steel was running back along the length of the boxcar. A PSF trooper from the other side of the train poked through between the two boxcars, and Steel shot him twice in the head.

Assault rifle fire poured toward the flatcar from the three Indians who were disguised as noncoms. A machine-gun emplacement aboard the flatcar was getting into action.

Holden dropped to one knee, the Beretta in both fists, Smith beside him, standing as erect as a duelist, his pistol extended at arm's length. They both opened fire against the two men behind the M-60 machine gun, Rosie already prone in front of them, firing at two guards on the roof of the second car. Holden kept shooting.

The machine gun fired one long burst. One of Twobears' men went down.

The machine gunner was dead.

So was the man with him.

One of the PSF men fired his M-16 as he ran across the flatcar toward the machine gun emplacement at its center.

Bob Twobears leaped up onto the flatcar and fired his pistol point-blank, about six shots, putting the PSF man down.

As Holden looked back toward the boxcar roofs, Steel was atop the third car, firing down into the flatcar.

Holden stood. Rosie was halfway up the ladder to the roof of the second boxcar, shot at a PSF man coming over the snow toward her. He fired his M-16, bullets ripping into the boxcar wall as Holden wheeled toward the man and fired. But the PSF trooper was already falling, his neck and left cheek covered in blood from Rosie's gunfire.

There were a few more sporadic shots. Then the shooting stopped.

Smith was on his belt radio. "This is Smith. Get down here, Harry, help us consolidate. Leave a half-dozen men at each end of the main street. Anybody in a PSF uniform you see who isn't one of us, kill him. Out."

Holden changed magazines in his pistol, shouted to Bob Twobears, "Release those personnel in the cattle cars, Bob, and get 'em loaded onto the trucks."

"Right!"

Holden bent down over the body of a dead PSF trooper, wiped the blood from his knife, sheathed it, walked on.

Rosie fell in beside Holden on his right, Charlie Thunderclap, the engineer, running up from the trucks, joining Holden on his left.

An engineer and a PSF officer, both men with hands raised high over their heads, were in the cab of the lead engine.

David Holden looked at the engineer. "Your services won't be required, engineer. Get down." And then Holden looked at the officer, a captain. "You in charge of this detail?"

"Yes, sir—what the hell's—"

"Shut up, or I'll do what logic tells me to do and blow

your brains all over the cab. Let me see your orders. Try anything and you're dead." Rosie jumped up into the cab through the open doorway, put the muzzle of her .45 beside the captain's left temple.

There was an embroidered name tag on the captain's field jacket. It read Jones. How imaginative! Holden thought.

Jones handed over his orders. . . .

"It was my first time in a real battle," Wisdom Twobears said, his eyes again drifting from his notes to the still-covered statue. "Randy Blumenthal, one of the FBI personnel who was a wanted man because he'd remained loyal to his assassinated President, his murdered Bureau director, and his chief, Luther Steel, kept me beside him all of the time. We hit it off as friends from the start, perhaps because, as the youngest agent from the old Metro unit, Randy was closest of all of them to my age. But also, I think, he kept me with him to keep me as safe as he could.

"My stepfather, Matthew Smith, was, of course, with Luther Steel and Professor David Holden and Rosie Shepherd Holden, the two leaders of the Metro Patriots and most active and most successful of the Patriot leaders until that time and since.

"Agent Blumenthal and myself, along with two dozen Native Americans, were holding one of the antiaircraft facilities the Patriots and Native American freedom fighters had taken over, this in anticipation of helicopters and possibly other types of airpower being employed against the train with which they intended to evacuate the kidnapped officers from Fort Makowski. We all know what happened, of course, yet we can never forget the sacrifices made that day."

CHAPTER THIRTY

*D*avid Holden ran through the less deep snow alongside the lead engine, looking back. The triangular shape of its three blazing yellow-white headlights against the deep blue of the snow-laden winter sky gave it the appearance of something out of one of the science fiction covers he used to draw for added money with which to better provide for Elizabeth and the children.

Rosie extended a hand from the train's cab, and Holden waited, ducked aside as the snowplow mounted forward of the main engine like a nineteenth-century cowcatcher sped past him, then he jumped aboard, snatching at her hand and the grab rail simultaneously.

No one pursued them from the town of Fort Devon, and nothing seemed out of the ordinary along the train's length.

At the diesel's throttle, Charlie Thunderclap gradually increased the RPMs.

The boxcars were emptied with the help of the townspeople, elements of the false floors laid in, then the Native American and Kalispell Patriot Cell personnel slid underneath, and the rest of the pieces set in.

From among the prisoners on the train in the two cattle cars, the hardiest were asked to come along, stay beside the exterior walls of the cattle cars, hiding still more of the Native American fighters.

As Holden looked again at Charlie Thunderclap, the engi-

neer announced, "I've disconnected the overspeed mechanism. Normally, it'd stop injection of fuel into the cylinders
if speed became too high. But I can control that manually so
we don't float something we shouldn't. Otherwise, there
could be an immediate engine shutdown, and we wouldn't
be able to restart with the trip reset lever until we had
dropped speed. That speed might be critical."

"Agreed." Holden nodded, slamming the door behind
him. Rosie was rubbing her gloved hands together. He
touched his lips to her forehead. "Relax."

"How long until we hit the fort?"

Holden looked at his watch. Then looked toward Thunderclap. "Twenty-five minutes?"

"Just about."

Smith's voice came in over the radio, and Holden responded. "this is Team Leader, reading you loud and clear.
Over."

"Just checking in. Everything back here is as it should be.
Over."

"Hang in there. Out." Holden hung up the microphone.
He looked at Rosie, then at Thunderclap. "Assuming all
goes well enough for us to be taking this train back down
the mountain, you have the second engine ready to go?"

"Breaking switch is in the Isolate position, all systems are
up and checked. We can really pour it on until we drop this
engine, and the second engine'll be ready to take the strain.
Remember, Professor, we'll be goin' downhill instead of up
like we are now."

Holden nodded.

He reached for Rosie's hand. She pulled off her glove,
nested her hand in his.

And he looked out the window.

The snow, if the sun had been shining, would have been
blindingly bright in its whiteness.

The higher they climbed into the mountains, the deeper the snow became, gradually encroaching, at last fully covering the gray gravel of the roadbed. Rising around them, ever more forbiddingly, toward the granite peaks through which the roadbed wound. At the base of the mountains and along some of the lower slopes, evergreen trees grew, their branches heavy-laden with snow, sagging under the weight.

As the locomotive took a curve, to their left was a stream, gunmetal gray and black, midnight blue edged ice on either side.

Holden held Rosie's hand more tightly. . . .

The attack came from where Randy Blumenthal had said it would likely originate, the slope below them and to the west. Wisdom Twobears had a captured M-16, taken from the body of one of the Presidential Strike Force men who had guarded the antiaircraft facility. He put the rifle to his shoulder, peering through the firing port.

He waited for the command from Randy Blumenthal.

He had never looked across the sights of a weapon at a man. His bowels felt a little loose, and his stomach churned. His hands sweated.

He could see from his limited perspective at least thirty men. He took his finger out of the rifle's trigger guard, flexed it, reinserted his finger, held it against the forwardmost portion of the trigger guard.

His breathing was erratic. He remembered Matthew always telling him, "The body is the platform from which the projectile is fired. The firearm, whatever it is, is only the launcher. If the platform is moving, no real accuracy is possible. And very often, Wisdom, the key to stabilizing that firing platform is breath control."

Wisdom Twobears forced himself to breathe more slowly.

Cold air through the firing port stung his face. He relished that because it heightened his perception. The firing ports had been blown out of the wall of the bunker with bits of plastic explosive hardly larger than a coin. They were ragged, but surprisingly uniform in size.

Wisdom saw more men now. What was wrong? Why wasn't Randy Blumenthal signaling that they should fire?

But Wisdom held his fire, waited, trusted.

His breathing was back under control, and the rifle shook almost not at all. He flexed his muscles to keep the circulation moving, to keep his arms and hands from starting to tremble.

And then his breath caught in his throat.

Randy Blumenthal gave the order. "Open fire!"

And Wisdom's finger moved almost independently of actual thought, just as his sights settled on a Presidential Strike Force officer charging toward the firing port.

As quickly as his finger moved, he pushed it forward, the rifle climbing only minimally in a short burst of four or five shots.

The PSF officer fell down.

Wisdom drew his cheek back from his rifle.

His body shook.

And then, as his vision started blurring with tears, he saw a PSF soldier dropping to one knee, two other soldiers flanking him. Something about the size of a long piece of pipe was going to the soldier's shoulder. And Wisdom realized that it was some kind of rocket launcher.

Wisdom sniffed back his tears, wiped his eyes against his coat sleeve, settled the sights of the rifle on the man with the rocket launcher.

He fired, the snow in front of the man with the rocket launcher plowing up, the man unharmed.

Gunfire poured toward Wisdom's firing port, concrete

dust spraying over his weapon, blowing toward his eyes. Holding higher this time, Wisdom Twobears fired again.

As he fired, the man's body seemed to lurch backward, and the rocket fired, but upward, a contrail of gray smoke behind it, then far off to the extreme right edge of Wisdom's peripheral vision, an explosion. It looked like several of the PSF soldiers fell victim to their own weapon.

Wisdom Twobears found another target. Another man. He fired. He hit the man the first time, killing him in an obvious way, blood spurting from the man's throat across the previously white snow.

Wisdom kept firing until his magazine was out, went over the changing procedure quickly in his head, removed the fired-out magazine, put a fresh one in place, returned to his firing port.

And now for the first time, he was aware of the cacophony around him, guns going off on all sides, explosions from the perimeter of the building.

And then at least one, perhaps both of the remote-controlled machine guns mounted on the bunker's dome opened fire, and enemy troops began falling almost in rows, like dominoes.

Wisdom kept firing. . . .

Thunderclap sat in the engineer's chair, his head inclined slightly out the right side window. "Professor! I've got the fort in sight."

David Holden looked at his wife, told her, "Give me a kiss, Rosie. I love you."

Rosie touched her hands to his face. "I love you, David."

His arms closed around her, and he held her tight as his mouth pressed down over hers.

If he could only think just of her for as long as a second, then whatever happened wouldn't matter that much.

CHAPTER THIRTY-ONE

*T*he highway, which had been paralleling their course for the previous twenty miles, at last linked with the roadbed for the rails as they passed out of the dank blackness of the short tunnel over which the northbound passed. The northbound lanes, two of them, were on the train's right, now, southbound lanes on the left. Snow was higher than a man's head on either side of each set of lanes, and the road was clear.

And several miles ahead lay the outer defenses of the fort, the ground already rising sharply toward Widow's Table, the peninsula of rock that extended over the canyon, at the farthest end of which were the high concrete block walls set with electrified barbed wire. Beyond these walls were the multistoried, interconnected blockhouses that formed the installation itself. Holden aimed his binoculars toward the fort. The deflection barriers were up across all four lanes of road and the tracks as well.

Beside Holden, Charlie Thunderclap was already slowing the train.

Rosie took her blackened Detonics .45 from beneath her BDU blouse and cocked the hammer, set the safety, and stashed it, along with her Glock-17, behind two six-packs of an offbrand cola inside the refrigerator. Holden looked at her as she turned away from the refrigerator. "Just in case." Rosie smiled.

The blade she'd adopted as her fighting knife—the Big Ugly One—was still on her pistol belt in its black sheath.

Holden glanced once again at the orders he'd taken from the PSF captain they'd left a prisoner of the townspeople in Fort Devon.

The train, bearing supplies and prisoners, was to enter Fort Makowski, offload both human and inanimate cargo, then immediately go back down for a rendezvous with a convoy of prisoners arriving this evening by train and truck in Helena. To meet such a schedule, offloading of the train would have to be expedited.

And hopefully, so would their entry past the outer guard stations.

Holden put the orders away. . . .

Bill Runningdeer moved along the dome of the bunker, his Uzi slung at his side. He kept low, gunfire coming toward him from three sides of the bunker now. One of the dome-mounted remote-controlled machine guns had been damaged beyond repair when the Patriots and their Indian allies had taken the facility. But the cover over the opening for the second gun was jammed. A large force of PSF personnel had attacked better than an hour ago and what existed now was a stalemate. But the PSF had the advantage, greater amounts of ammunition and higher numbers of personnel; the more protracted the conflict, the greater the chance that the PSF would win.

The remote-controlled machine gun could sway the odds in favor of the Patriots and the Indians.

Runningdeer neared the summit of the dome, dropped there, tucking back as gunfire from the Presidential Strike Force attackers zigzagged across the concrete surface just ahead of him.

Runningdeer swung the Uzi forward.

He waited for what he hoped was a lull, then started up the dome, slipping, gunfire hammering into the concrete beside him, spraying his face with snow and concrete dust. He pushed himself up, the back of his right hand bleeding, but no time to worry over it.

He clambered along the dome's surface, keeping his body as flat against it as he could.

A bullet tore through his left thigh, and Runningdeer slipped, fell back, skidding down the dome, pawing at the surface with both hands, slowing himself, stopping.

He looked down at his left thigh. The snow and concrete around his leg were already reddening with blood. "Shit," Bill Runningdeer snarled.

He rolled onto his back, tore away part of his trouser leg, bound it over the wound tightly, his eyes shutting against the pain, teeth gritted.

More gunfire, from about fifty yards to the north. Runningdeer extended the Uzi's stock, brought the submachine gun to his shoulder, and fired a short burst, then again. As answering fire came, Runningdeer sprayed out the Uzi's thirty-two-round magazine in long bursts toward the source of the gunfire. He saw a man fall.

Letting the empty magazine fall away down the dome, he rammed a fresh one—this time a twenty—up the well, then started to climb again.

He neared the height of the dome now, gunfire rippling over the concrete and snow, churning up waves of dust and ice spicules. He drew back. Just ahead of him, he could see the cover for the firing port. It was jammed half open.

Runningdeer pulled the magazine from the Uzi, let the bolt forward, remagazined. He started climbing again.

A bullet creased across his back, and he fell flat, cursing against the pain. But he hadn't slid back.

Runningdeer shook his head to clear it.

He'd been the classic case they made TV movies about, essentially a delinquent, growing up too poor and too tough on a reservation, dropping out of school.

He'd never quite figured what turned him around, but he went back, finished school, finished college, applied for the Federal Bureau of Investigation, always secretly thought that he was accepted merely to meet some quota for nonwhites.

But all the pieces had fallen together for him. It was work he loved—second only to his country.

Runningdeer started climbing again, collapsed beside the jammed door for the machine gun's firing port. He swung the Uzi around, getting the folded-out stock's buttplate beneath the jammed door, pushing in farther, then throwing his body weight upward against the door, using the Uzi's stock as a crowbar.

The door didn't budge.

Runningdeer got his right knee bent, his left leg no longer responding. He pushed with all his strength.

There was a snapping sound, the firing port door flying open.

As Runningdeer half knelt there, poised over it, he felt the bullet in his back.

And he started to fall, the Uzi flying from his grasp, his left shoulder impacting the ridge at the base of the dome, an ear-splitting crack, and he was falling through the air.

He fell onto his back and screamed with the pain, snow all around him, virtually covering him.

As he turned his head—it hurt to move—one of the Presidential Strike Force troopers rushed toward him, a bayonet fixed to his M-16. As the man lunged to finish him, Bill Runningdeer smiled.

In his right hand, Runningdeer held the butt of the SIG-

Sauer P-226 from his belt. He'd grabbed for it when he took the fall, hadn't lost it.

He heard the remote-operated machine gun opening up from the top of the bunker. It would turn the tide of battle.

The PSF trooper with the bayonet looked like a thousand other sociopathic street punks he'd seen at the scenes of crime, in line ups, in mug shots, on morgue slabs.

Bill Runningdeer raised the 9mm and fired twice into the PSF trooper's neck and face, telling him, "You lose real big this time, asshole."

Runningdeer felt a sharp pain along his spine, and the pain seemed to sweep across the top of his head. His limbs began to spasm. The pistol fell from his hand. He murmured, "God."

And then the pain in Bill Runningdeer's head exploded, and he closed his eyes.

CHAPTER THIRTY-TWO

*T*he deflection barriers were lowered as the corporal of the outer guard returned the orders to David Holden's hand. "Thank you, sir."

Holden returned his salute.

At the controls of the engine, Charlie Thunderclap let out the throttle, and they started slowly ahead, between the wired enclosures on either side, beyond which lay land mines and other booby traps.

Holden looked at his watch. He looked at Rosie.

He looked ahead, the inner gates still closed. If this Lieutenant Colonel Hackler were a really clever tactician, he'd keep the inner gates closed so the train would be forced to stop, try to back out, then spring his trap.

Holden hoped Hackler wasn't that clever.

The gates began to open.

Beside him, Holden heard his wife—his wife—he heard her let out a long sigh.

At the outer guard station, Steel and Smith and some of the others had climbed aboard the roofs of the boxcars and the cattle cars in which the prisoners were hauled.

That was standard procedure for the PSF, Holden had observed.

The gates were fully opened now, and Holden could see what looked like normal activity inside the walls. Guards patrolled the tops of the walls behind the electrified barbed wire, but in no greater numbers than Holden had observed the myriad times he had watched trains enter and leave since his first arrival here.

All this normalcy bothered Holden, made him more certain than ever that there was a trap laid for them.

The series of interconnected multistoried blockhouses was easier than ever to see in detail. The buildings were prefabricated, but sturdy seeming, even those that appeared isolated, linked by low, rounded tunnels resembling entrances to igloos.

Thunderclap began to slow the train again, the end of the tracks ahead.

Again, if Hackler were clever, the tracks behind them could have been mined. That way, the train would be trapped inside.

The airbrakes were screeching, the sound like some wild creature in agony. But the agony passed and the train stopped.

"Be ready," Holden hissed to Thunderclap.

As Holden threw back the door and started to step down, three men emerged from the central building of the complex. Holden's observations had confirmed what local intelligence information supported, that this was the command structure for Fort Makowski.

Holden didn't wait for the three men to reach him. Already, some of his own personnel, mostly Indians, but all in PSF battle dress utilities and field jackets, were beginning to get down from the roofs of the cars, the remainder coming out of the large caboose at the end.

Holden shouted to Smith, who was atop the lead boxcar. "Sergeant, give the order to unload the prisoners!"

"Yes, sir!"

Smith shouted back along the cars, "Begin unloading. Let's move it out!"

Rosie jumped down from the train. Holden eyed the three men advancing toward him again, all three officers, all three under sidearms only. Holden turned to Rosie, "Lieutenant, supervise the unloading. Get every one of those scum who can carry anything to move the prisoners who can't walk and then start on those boxcars." Under his breath, Holden added, "And keep your fingers crossed, sweetheart."

Rosie gave him a quick wink, saluted. He returned it. She walked off. Under other circumstances, he would have been amused, seeing her trying to walk like a man.

But he turned away, toward the three officers, now about ten yards from him.

At five yards, all three men stopped. The man at the center wore the insignia of a lieutenant colonel. Hackler. But Hackler did not salute.

Instead, he called out, "Whoever you are, sir, your withdrawal is now impossible. The tracks behind you have been mined. Should you attempt to move this train, the mines will be detonated."

The game was up, but they were inside, the best Holden had ever hoped for as far as any sort of ruse was concerned.

Holden called back to him, "You are Lieutenant Colonel Hackler?"

"That is correct. Your name, sir?"

"I am David Holden."

Hackler hesitated a moment, then returned, "I had anticipated your arrival, sir. You are to lay down your arms and order your personnel to do the same. Otherwise, they will be fired upon."

Holden looked to the gray concrete walls surrounding him. They bore a striking resemblance to the walls surrounding prisons in 1930's movies. Holden looked again at Hackler. "One of the boxcars, Colonel, is packed from floor to ceiling and side to side with high explosives and combustible fluids." That was true, but they were heavier on the combustible fluids. "At my order, or the order of any of my senior personnel, that combination will be detonated. All of us standing here, all your personnel on the eastern wall, will be killed. Even the wall itself will be destroyed, as will the interior gates. The explosion should be powerful enough to detonate the majority of the mines set between the inner and outer perimeters. The resultant explosion could destroy better than fifty percent of your facility."

Hackler didn't answer for a moment, then smiled. "But, sir, my primary mission would be accomplished: your death."

David Holden smiled back. "Colonel, I admire your resoluteness. In the interest of common decency, before we attempt to resolve this matter, I respectfully request that the prisoners aboard the cattle cars be allowed to remove themselves from the field and to the west wall."

Hackler said nothing for a moment, then, "I cannot grant that request, Dr. Holden."

Holden was only trying to buy time, time for the personnel under the false flooring in the other two boxcars to be ready to fight, but if he could get the prisoners and his own personnel who were mixed in with them to the far wall, so much the better. He continued on this tack. "I must insist that whoever has such authority be summoned."

Hackler said nothing.

Holden continued. "I am aware of the fact that Roman Makowski and Hobart Townes are present at this facility." His latest intelligence data confirmed Townes with certainty, Makowski's presence a better than fifty percent chance.

"The President, here?"

Now Holden was certain. "Yes, Colonel. I had not anticipated your mining the tracks behind us. You have me at a disadvantage. If you allow the prisoners to withdraw from the cattle cars to the west wall, I will discuss terms."

Holden had been counting seconds. By now, the majority of the personnel aboard the cattle cars—about three dozen actual prisoners and the rest, twice that number, Native American personnel armed with handguns, grenades, and knives—should be on the ground.

By now, too, the boxcar false floors would be raising, personnel armed with the G-3s and M-16s Rosie had flown in with and additional M-16s liberated from the PSF in Fort Devon, ready to move.

Hackler spoke, "Either surrender now, Professor Holden, or we will detonate the train tracks and open fire."

Holden looked back along the length of the train. "My boxcar loaded with explosives is close enough to the end of the train, Colonel, that I may not have to order detonation myself. Your explosives may detonate it for me." And he looked at Hackler and smiled. "Your move."

Hackler seemed to be studying his face. After a long pause, Hackler reached for his belt radio. Holden was ready to draw down on him. But Hackler said into his radio, "Mr. Townes, this is Hackler. Professor Holden claims to have the last boxcar filled with explosives and says that he is prepared to detonate the explosives and flammable liquids if the prisoners from the cattle cars are not allowed to withdraw to the west wall. What should I do, sir?"

Holden felt himself smiling.

Hackler held the earpiece for the radio by the side of his head.

Hackler's face read like a book. The corners of Hackler's mouth downturned in something that was at once a combination of sadness and disgust. He let the earpiece drop, turned his eyes toward Holden.

Holden didn't wait for the reply. He already knew what it

would be. Men like Hobart Townes and Roman Makowski had a preset number of responses, and none of those incorporated compassion, reason, or anything similar.

Holden shouted, "Now!" as he dodged right and back, tugging the full-sized Beretta from the fabric full-flap uniform holster at his right side.

Holden's thumb worked the safety up as the first gunfire came, some of it from the tops of the boxcars, some of it from the wall. A bullet grazed across Holden's left bicep. Holden stabbed the pistol toward the three PSF officers. Hackler's gun was already out too. Holden and Hackler fired simultaneously.

There was a burning sensation across Holden's left thigh, then a feeling of icy cold as Hackler's body swayed, then blood spurted from Hackler's throat, and Hackler fell over dead.

The sound of the Hawk MM-1 firing, gas grenades exploding all over the quadrangle.

The heavy reports of G-3s, their 7.62mm ammunition easily distinguishable from the 5.56mm rounds of the M-16s. Holden dropped to one knee, edging back beside the diesel, Thunderclap firing an H & K submachine gun into the other two retreating PSF officers. Holden drew back under the diesel, pulled his gas mask from the bag at his side, tore the beret from his head, pulled on the mask, exhaled, popped the cheeks of the mask, inhaled. The rubbery smell was always nauseating to him on the first breath. But it beat tear gas.

Neither wound he had sustained was much of a bleeder.

As he started from beneath the diesel, Holden looked on the other side. PSF personnel were rappeling down from the eastern wall.

"Shit," Holden snarled. He reached under his BDU for the second, smaller Beretta in the shoulder holster there.

The larger Beretta in his left hand, the compact in his right, Holden rolled across the track bed beneath the engine and came up on one knee, both 9mms firing in tandem, cutting down the rappeling PSF personnel.

Gunfire tore into the ground to his right, and he fell away from it, swung both pistols on line, found his target on the top of the eastern wall, fired both pistols simultaneously. The man's body fell back into the electrified barbed wire, electricity arcing across his body, smoke rising from his face and his clothing.

Holden was up, his left leg stinging a little as he ran, but not badly.

Another rappeler. Holden shot him dead, running toward the man, safing both pistols as he stuffed them into his field jacket pockets, grabbing up the dead man's M-16. Holden sprayed it out across the top of the wall, killing five more of the PSF troopers. The M-16 empty, he was about to throw it down. One of the PSF men from the wall flung himself downward, Holden taking the brunt of the man's fall, the man rolling off him, past him, coming up like a cat on all fours, then drawing a pistol.

No time for anything else, David Holden took the M-16 in both fists and swung, catching the PSF man across the bridge of the nose with the M-16's flash deflector, blood spurting everywhere.

At the far left edge of his peripheral vision, Holden saw movement, wheeled and dodged back, another of the PSF men charging him, rifle butt turned toward Holden's face.

Holden inverted the rifle in his own hands and swung, catching the trooper across the right side of the head. Holden wheeled toward the first man, the rifle still held like a club in Holden's hands. He smashed the butt down across the top of the man's head, the rifle butt shattering, more blood spurting from the top of the man's head.

Holden took a step back, drew his pistols.

Gas was filtering toward this side of the train now, in huge, billowing gray clouds.

The sounds of 40mm grenades now, the Hawk MM-1 firing again.

Three PSF personnel were clambering up toward the roof of the first boxcar. Holden fired his pistols, the slides locking open on empty as one of the men fell.

Ramming both pistols into his belt, slides still locked back, Holden dug for the Desert Eagle under his shirt. "Smith! Behind you!"

Holden cleared the Desert Eagle from his clothing, jacked back the slide, and fired, blowing another of the men off the ladder. As Holden brought the muzzle onto the third man, Smith appeared at the edge of the roof, his Beretta 92F in his right hand. He shot the third man through the forehead, the body tumbling back from the ladder.

Holden ran for the break between the boxcar and the second engine, clambered up the hydraulic lines and the coupling. Fighting was general in the quadrangle now, the men and few women from the cattle cars, prisoners and American Indian volunteers alike, fighting at close quarters against what seemed a never-ending stream of fully armed PSF personnel coming from the network of concrete blockhouses. But the Indians and military officers had only handguns and knives to fight against assault rifles.

Holden scanned the tops of the boxcars, saw Bob Twobears with the MM-1. "Twobears! Fire on the personnel exiting the blockhouses. Now!"

Twobears shot Holden a wave, closed the MM-1, and fired, his first grenade impacting about twenty-five yards from the front of the nearest blockhouse, into a cluster of perhaps a dozen PSF personnel, killing or wounding all of them.

Rosie was suddenly beside Holden, handing him a G-3 and a musette bag of spare magazines. He safed the G-3, found a niche for it in his waistband. "Locked and loaded, David!"

"Right!" Holden, his wife Rosie beside him, ran toward the command building, shouting to Steel, Smith down from the boxcar roof and beside Steel now. "Luther! Get about two dozen men with us. We're going after Makowski and Townes! Send another two dozen toward the prison cells. We can arm the prisoners who can still fight!"

Holden waited until he got a signal of acknowledgment from Steel, then ran on, Rosie beside him. The wound in his left bicep hurt more now than the wound in his thigh. But neither hurt badly, nor yet seemed to be bleeders.

Holden called off a half dozen of the personnel from the boxcars, getting them with him and Rosie as they reached the doors of the command center.

The doors were heavy, but not armored. Holden tried a kick. Nothing happened. He fired a burst toward the lock mechanism. Nothing but ricochets whining dangerously near them. "Nuts!" Holden grabbed for his radio. "Twobears! Twobears! This is Holden. Twobears!"

"Whatcha want?"

"Fire into the doors here. Do it fast."

"Get back!"

Holden pouched the radio, shouted to Rosie and the men around them. "Get away from the doors. Hide under anything, dead men, anything!"

Holden grabbed Rosie, running with her from the doors, doing exactly what he'd advised. There were three dead PSF troopers nearby, and Holden let his rifle fall to his side on its sling, grabbed at one body, hauled it onto one of the others, Rosie grabbing for the third. They threw it atop the other two, Holden grabbing Rosie, pulling her down. Holden covered her head with his own body, the three dead men shielding them as well.

An explosion, then another, then another, Holden's ears ringing with them.

Twobears' voice over the radio; Holden had the volume maxed. "We got the door!"

"Roger that. Keep working on the men coming out of the buildings." Holden was up, Rosie beside him, the G-3 in one hand, the Desert Eagle in the other, Rosie with a G-3. The others who had been with them, and now Steel and Smith and over twenty men, joined them as they charged the blown-out doors of the command center.

This was the largest of the buildings and, with the exception of the prison structures, probably the most impregnable.

Steel and Smith and three others sprayed their G-3s through the open doorway. Rosie reached out a gas grenade from her musette bag, lobbed it, pulled the pin on another, and bowled it in afterward.

"Sound and light!" Holden ordered.

Steel pulled the pin on one, shouted, "Everybody back!" He hurtled it through the doorway. There was a high-pitched whistling Holden could still hear even with his right shoulder raised to his right ear, his left hand, still holding the Desert Eagle, over his left.

He counted the seconds, opened his eyes, shouted, "One more gas and we go!"

Rosie pitched the third gas grenade and Holden shouted, "Now!" He ran through the doorway the instant after the grenade went, the cloud of gas swirling around him, his gas mask saving him from its effect.

A PSF trooper, coughing, gagging, firing a pistol blindly, opened up on him. Holden shot him in the chest with the Desert Eagle, dropping him.

Rosie on his right now, Steel and Smith and the others behind them, Holden moved along the corridor at a jog, noting overturned desks, papers strewn everywhere about. Even an army of homicidal criminals had its reports to file.

Each office they passed was empty of personnel.

At the end of the corridor, there was a staircase. "Luther, take the first floor, secure it, hold it. Smith. Same for the second."

"Right!"

Holden started up the stairs, calling to the twenty-six or so men with them. "You and you and you and you, come with us!"

They reached the first landing, Smith and his party breaking off, Smith lobbing a gas grenade through an open door.

Holden, despite the wound in his thigh, took the next set of steps two at a time, Rosie running beside him, the four men just behind them.

There was a door at the head of the landing, metal, closed shut.

Holden reached out to Rosie. "Got that adhesive tape?"

"Right."

They moved toward the door, Holden shouting to the others, "Keep the stairs below us covered and take shelter away from the door." Rosie fed out a strip of the wide surgical adhesive, pressing it fast against one side of the doorframe. Holden took a grenade from her bag, slid the spoon over the tape, the grenade body under it, right beside the joint. She ran the strip across the width of the door, Holden setting a second grenade, where the door met the frame. "We'll be coming fast. Give us room on the stairs!"

Rosie looked at him. She took hold of one of the cotter pins.

Holden took the other one as she dropped the unused tape into her bag. "Count of three, Rosie! One. Two.

Three!" Holden and Rosie simultaneously pulled the pins, running, the spoons clattering against the metal doors, Rosie dropping to her knees, skidding, rolling over the edge of the landing, Holden grabbing for the rail, jumping, coming down hard, going flat.

There was a roar so loud that for a moment Holden thought his eardrums would rupture; shards of shrapnel from the metal door flew everywhere, the man beside Holden, one of the freed officers, Navy, taking one in his leg.

Holden pushed himself up, shouted at the top of his lungs, "See to this man! Rest of you! Let's go!" Holden, Rosie beside him, dodged around the debris, racing toward the demolished doorway. Rosie flung a gas grenade through, Holden firing the G-3 out. They fanned themselves on both sides of what was left of the doorway.

Rosie screamed, "Sound and light!" Holden looked away, covered his ears. The whine rose and fell. Holden opened his eyes, looked back, rammed a fresh magazine up the well of the G-3.

The man with the shrapnel wound shouted, "I'm coverin' ya!"

Holden shot him a wave, then shouted to Rosie and the men, "Let's go!"

Holden fired a short burst, Rosie the same, at angles to each other. They went through.

Gunfire tore into the corridor wall near them from the far end of the floor. Holden started to tell Rosie to use a grenade, but she shouted, "Outgoing grenade!"

Holden pulled back, Rosie beside him.

As the grenade blew, the floor under them shook, and a false wall to their left collapsed toward them. Rosie drew back, Holden beside her.

Plaster dust was thick in the air, but the mask would filter it.

And there was smoke. A fire.

Holden rallied the three men with them. "When I say fire, pour everything you can into that far section. When I say hold your fire, do it."

Holden dropped prone in the dust and debris, Rosie beside and a little behind him. The others were in position. Gunfire originated from the far end of the floor again, perhaps a washroom.

Holden shouted, "Fire!"

Simultaneously, all five of them opened fire with their rifles, chunks of the far wall shredding away, chairs and desks dancing along the floor under the multiple impacts, then suddenly disintegrating. Holden changed magazines, kept firing. The door beside the point of origin for the assault rifle fire directed at them fell off its hinges. Pieces of the far wall were crumbling.

Holden put a fresh magazine up the G-3's well, shouted as loud as he could, the noise deafening, "Cease fire! Cease fire!"

There was gunfire from the floor below them, but no more here.

Holden got up into a crouch, telling Rosie and the others, "Fan out, and be careful!" The Desert Eagle went to his left hand.

Rosie, her G-3 in her right hand, held a Beretta 92F in the left. She moved to his far right.

Holden's eyes stayed on the far wall, a washroom complex almost definitely.

A dead body behind an overturned desk.

A long, ragged blood stain across the floor, a dead body at its end, behind a row of filing cabinets.

Holden reached the far wall.

He took cover behind an overturned metal desk. Rosie and the others took cover as well. Holden shouted, "Anybody alive in there, listen." He almost smiled at the silliness of his phrasing. "Come out or we blow you out. Move it!"

And there was a voice coming back almost instantly. "Don't! Please! I'm the only one and I'm trapped."

Holden snarled under his breath through the mask, "Right."

The voice came again, and somehow it sounded familiar. "Please don't hurt me! I'll give you anything you want!"

Holden stood, Rosie standing too, the others still behind cover.

They flanked the doorway. "Gas," Holden told her.

Rosie nodded, pulled a grenade from her bag. "Last one."

"Use it anyway."

Rosie plucked out the pin, rolled the grenade through the doorway as Holden fired a burst into the ceiling just inside. There was a shriek. "Please don't hurt me!"

Now Holden knew.

The grenade went off, a gas cloud billowing back toward them.

Holden went through left to right, Rosie right to left.

"Gee whiz! A men's room!"

Holden looked at the far wall, urinals hanging half off it, water spraying across the floor from ruptured pipes. And he was embarrassed. "Get outta here."

"Relax!"

Holden shook his head, started forward.

The voice again. "Please! I can give you anything you want!"

Holden went forward, Rosie on the opposite wall. As he crossed around the side of a stall, kneeling in an inch or two of water, hugging a toilet bowl for protection, his left leg bloodied and one pant leg torn, was the man who called himself a President.

"You're a bad joke, Makowski, but you just might get us out of here."

Rosie spit at him.

Holden shouted to the men behind them, "Help this thing, see to his wound and we're outta here!"

Roman Makowski still hugged his toilet bowl like a man might hug a woman. . . .

Over the radio, Bob Twobears said, "We've got about a hundred of them boxed up in their barracks, but they're fully equipped. Our men on the wall report a dozen or more half-tracks coming up along the road with PSF markings. Could be what's left from the people who would have left the fort to hit the antiaircraft installations."

Holden was nearly to the base of the stairs as he said into the radio, "Get the explosives in the boxcar neutralized quickly, get the more powerful stuff into the lead engine. Get ready to roll the jellied gasoline out as required. Over."

"We've got most of the prisoners who could walk loaded. The rest are being carried onto the boxcars. We were able to arm about a hundred of them. But we're going to be standing-room only. There were a lot more personnel here than we figured. Over."

"Speed it up, Bob. Out."

Holden walked into the first-floor corridor, Rosie beside him, Roman Makowski between two of the men, the injured Naval officer hobbling along beside the remaining man.

Smith and two of his men were there, covering the main-floor entrance. "We killed everyone we saw. But a number of them were dead already. Townes shot himself in the head."

"Let's go," Holden told him.

They moved along the corridor, past the debris, toward the quadrangle.

As they walked out into the air, Holden pulled off his

mask, the gas clouds dissipated. Smoke curled from the roofs of several of the blockhouses.

The quadrangle was teeming with men helping other men and women, released prisoners, toward the train.

Holden called Twobears on the radio. "Bob. David here. How long on those trucks? Over."

"Our guys on the outside are engaging them now. But they won't be able to hold them. They're coming up both sides of the road. Maybe ten or twelve minutes. Over."

"As soon as we're rolling, tell your people on the outside to disengage and split up and run for it. The PSF will stick with us, not them. Get us set to detonate those mine fields on both sides of the entrance as we leave. You've got five minutes to get some charges set in this place that'll do the most damage. Rosie and Luther know how. Get 'em some people. Out."

Holden pouched the radio.

He looked at Rosie. She was so pretty. "Get on with the explosives. I'm going to the train. And gimme a cigarette." She lit one for him, handed it to him, smiled.

As she ran off, her rifle at high port, Holden shouted behind him to Smith. "Matthew. Help Bob with loading up the train. We're almost out of time."

"Agreed." And Smith took off at a run toward the train.

Holden let his rifle fall to his side on its sling. He put a fresh magazine into the Desert Eagle, pocketing the partially spent one, safely lowered the pistol's hammer, belted the gun.

He changed magazines in both Berettas, returning the larger one to the flap holster at his right hip, the smaller one to the shoulder holster beneath his jacket.

The cigarette in the right corner of his mouth, he walked toward the train, calling to the men with him, "I'll keep an eye on Makowski. Help in the loading." Holden grasped the

G-3 at the pistol grip, pointed it at Makowski. "I won't kill you if you run, but I'll hurt you."

Time was becoming a more intractable enemy than the Presidential Strike Force. . . .

As they reversed out of the quadrangle, David Holden looked at the floor of the engine compartment. Sitting there, hands behind his head because there'd been no time to tie him, was Roman Makowski.

Holden looked away in disgust.

Makowski said, "I can give you Townes's job, Professor. I've always admired your courage. You have the charisma of leadership. Think about the power, the wealth, this entire nation, all of it to share with me."

"You'll be too busy being tried for treason as soon as this country's back on its feet. Treason, murder, probably charges no one has even considered."

"I'm offering you and your mistress—"

"Wife," Rosie corrected.

"You and your wife, then, I'm offering you life as opposed to death, luxury as opposed to living on the run and hiding, all the power anyone could ever dream of."

David Holden didn't look at Roman Makowski. He looked at Rosie. "Tell him our decision."

Rosie looked at Makowski. "Shut the fuck up or I'll knee-cap you, you son of a bitch."

Holden laughed.

They were into the ground between the inner and outer perimeters, the mine fields on either side of them. Bob Twobears' voice came over the radio. "My guys are pulling back. They can't hold out any longer. Over."

"They bought us enough time," Holden lied. "Make sure they split up so the PSF follows us. Out." Holden looked at Smith. "See if you can raise the PSF on that radio." And

Holden gestured toward the radio that was mounted in the engineer's compartment.

Smith cocked his eyebrows, nodded.

Holden raised Twobears again. "Bob. Over."

"Readin' you, David. Over."

"Tell Luther to be ready to detonate the tracks behind us and the mine fields on my signal. Keep the frequency open. Over."

"Standing by. Over."

Smith said, "I've got the PSF force that's coming up the road. A Captain Vargas."

Holden nodded, handed Rosie the one microphone and took the other. "Captain Vargas. This is David Holden. Townes and Hackler are dead. We have a heavily armed force. And we're holding Roman Makowski hostage. Over."

"Confirm that, Holden."

Holden shrugged his shoulders, nodded toward Makowski.

Makowski got to his feet stiffly, dragging his bandaged left leg as if it were broken. It was a flesh wound from a piece of shrapnel, the bleeding stopped and a painkiller administered.

Holden handed Makowski the microphone. "Talk to the man. Tell him we're holding you and we'll kill you if they attack. We won't, unless they're about to overrun us, but Rosie can always show you what she meant by kneecapping."

"What if I say no?"

David Holden drew the Desert Eagle from his belt, thumbed back the hammer, pointed the gun at Makowski's face so he could see the size of the bore, then lowered it, aiming it at Makowski's right knee. "I can kneecap you too. Rosie can have the other knee."

Makowski took the microphone. "This is the President. Do not attempt to attack this train. Do you understand me? They will kill me. You are ordered to stay back."

Holden took the microphone as the return transmission came. "You stupid son of a bitch, lettin' yourself get caught. Let 'em kill you, or we will." The transmission went dead. Makowski's face went white.

Holden shrugged his shoulders.

Smith said, "I'll raise Steinmetz Air Force Base. They should be scrambled by now."

Holden nodded.

"That insolent—" Makowski began.

Holden looked at him, looked away. "Gimme a cigarette, Rosie, huh?"

She lit one for him, handed it to him, lit one for herself. Holden waited.

Smith was still calling out.

At last, Smith said, "I've got them."

Holden checked their position. They were well past the other side of the deflection barriers now. He took the other microphone from Rosie. "Bob, this is David. Tell Luther to blow all explosives in and around the fort now. Over."

"I understand. Out."

Holden racked the microphone, then took the other microphone from Smith. "To whom am I speaking? Over."

"This is Lieutenant Colonel Thomas Fullerton, commander of the fighter wing closing currently on your position, hostile force. Over."

"From Steinmetz? Over."

"That is correct. You are ordered to stay right where you are and make visible signs of laying down your arms. Over."

"We can't do that. Stand by for an important message, please. Over." Holden handed the microphone to Makowski, saying, "Try for a better public image this time, Roman."

Makowski licked his lips. "This, this is Roman Makowski, the President. I am ordering you to turn back. I am being held captive by these people, who will kill me if you do not."

The fighter leader's voice came back. "I'm sorry, Mr. President, but I must somehow confirm that you are who you claim to be. Over."

Holden took the microphone. "Check with Washington. Try Townes's office. We'll be busy enough with the folks on the ground who are trying to kill us. The PSF convoy leader, a Captain Vargas, has indicated that he will attack and force us to kill Makowski. Your base commander should be able to confirm that Makowski was at the fort named after him. Townes shot himself, Makowski is captured, the base commander, Eugene Hackler, is dead, the base all but destroyed. I am David Holden of the Patriots. Call us back unless you want Makowski's death on your hands. Out."

"No, wait a minute, Dr. Holden. We're breaking off. Good luck. Out."

Holden smiled, returned the microphone to Smith.

The explosion began, a ripple effect along both sides of the tracks between the two walls, then the tracks themselves near the interior boundary, then some of the buildings, collapsing in on themselves as puffs of gray smoke rose from shot-out windows.

Makowski said, "What are you doing now?"

"We're going to get up all the speed we can, outdistance your PSF friends—Captain Vargas—then use demolitions along the road so they can't follow. Just sit down and stay out of the way, and you'll live to stand trial so long as we live. And I promise you that, by the way, it'll be a fair trial. More than anyone would get at your hands."

Rosie grabbed Makowski by the collar, jerked him back. "Over there and shut up!"

Holden looked to Charlie Thunderclap. "With both engines, how long will we be parallel to them?"

"Maybe three minutes if they're smart."

Holden nodded. He had assumed from the outset that with one experienced engineer only the most intelligent man among them was the best man to assume control of the second engine during the moments prior to transfer and separation in lieu of a second engineer. That man was obviously Matthew Smith. There were ropes rigged along the outside of both engines to facilitate the transfer from one engine to another. He looked at Smith. "Matthew. Go back into the second engine and go through the GP38-2 Operator's Manual procedures again. We'll be separating shortly."

Smith nodded, saying nothing. For some reason, as Smith passed him, Holden stopped the man, extended his hand. Smith took it, looking at him oddly. Then Smith said, "A pleasure, sir. A true pleasure." And Smith started out through the door, onto the ropes.

Twobears' voice came over the radio. "David, we're about two minutes now from closing with the PSF convoy. We're ready with the jellied gasoline and explosives, and everybody we can get to a position that can be fired from is ready. Over."

"Smith's coming forward, preparatory to separation. Hang in there. Out."

Holden limped toward the explosives that were situated near the nose of the diesel. The rigging was hurried and crude, but once the explosives were detonated, they'd do the job—he hoped. . . .

* * *

Half-track trucks painted after the pattern of the Presidential Strike Force were on the top of the tunnel and on both sides of the road, waiting for them.

Rose Holden started out onto the ropes, Charlie Thunderclap already nearing the spare engine, David at the controls of the primary engine.

Some rifle fire, the distance still too great to be anything but harassing fire, was already coming toward them.

Between her and Charlie Thunderclap was Roman Makowski.

She knew the plan, hated it, but realized its effectiveness.

As soon as David was certain they were across, he would match speeds with the second engine, sever the lines linking the two diesels, then follow them. Once David had transferred to the spare engine, that engine would increase speed under the hands of Charlie Thunderclap. Meanwhile, the primary engine's braking system would kick in, slowing it.

The explosives contained in the primary engine's nose would be triggered by radio signal so the engine would explode beneath the tunnel, thereby bringing the tunnel down and effectively sealing off the road and the tracks behind them, giving them a clear run to Fort Devon, where reinforcements and transportation awaited them.

Makowski was nearly to the end of the primary engine.

Charlie Thunderclap had already transferred.

Rose shouted to Makowski. "Let's move, Roman!"

And then Makowski did something she had never thought he would do. He showed that he had a spine. Makowski flung himself from the ropes to which they clung, hurtling his body toward her.

Rose Holden's right hand lost its grip as Makowski's body impacted her. Her right hand slipped from the rope as she shouted, "David!" Makowski's hands were on the rope, both of them. With his injured left leg, he kicked toward her, again and again, into her left breast, her abdomen. "David!"

But the slipstream was too loud.

And gunfire now was pouring from the vehicles on both sides of the road.

Luther would be releasing the jellied gasoline from the boxcar roofs.

Just as the thought came to her, the first of the fifty-five gallon drums was hurtled down, a burst of assault rifle poured into it, the jellied gasoline exploding.

There was a rush of heat as she clung there with one hand to the rope, her feet flying free, Makowski kicking at her belly.

The baby.

Fire scorched near her and she felt she could not breathe.

Makowski's left hand hammered at her left hand, pounded against her wrist, her forearm.

He kicked at her abdomen again, and she lost her grip, reaching out with her right hand, catching Makowski's right leg at the ankle. Rose swung her left hand up, her legs dragging over the snow and gravel.

Gunfire hammered into the locomotive's body.

Makowski kicked at her face, Rose's left cheek taking a glancing blow. Her right hand lost its grip as he dragged himself toward the front of the primary engine, clambering over the ropes.

Rose hung there, her boots shredding away, her left breast and her stomach cramping.

Tears streamed down her face, drying as quickly as they appeared, the slipstream around the train overpoweringly strong.

Another drum of jellied gasoline was exploded.

Rose swung her right arm up, caught the rope in her

hand, let the full power of the drag swing her legs upward, catching her right leg into the bottom rope.

Her face hung inches above the snow and gravel of the railbed now. Searing heat washed over her from the fiery gasoline.

Gunfire came from every boxcar door, every rooftop, every break between the bars of the cattle cars.

And return fire came from the PSF convoy.

As she clung to the lower rope, a bullet tore through her left forearm, and she screamed, losing her grip, her arm numbed.

She hung there, the pain and the sickening heat swallowing her.

"Damn you!" Rose Holden swung her injured arm up, getting her elbow over the lower rope, twisting her body upward, the rope gouging into her now as she straddled it. And she realized she was screaming with pain.

She hugged the rope that tortured her, then snapped her right arm up, grasping for the upper rope. She had it.

Coming from the spare engine now, along the ropes to make the jump to the primary engine, she saw Matthew Smith. He was shouting to her.

As she started to scream back to him, the engines separated.

Smith was thrown back, clung to the ropes, tried edging along them, but the primary engine's wheels were screeching. It was starting to change gears, breaking with its wheels. Smith hung there at the front of the spare engine, reaching, but the gap suddenly widening.

Rose Holden clung to the ropes.

If the engines were separating, Makowski had gotten David.

She was bleeding heavily and cramps wrenched through

her body. But she took one last look at Matthew Smith, then started out along the ropes, toward the compartment.

Only her right hand could move, and each time she dragged her left arm over the rope, a new spasm of pain shot through her.

She looked onto the road. They were even with the PSF vehicles, nearly under the tunnel, the engine not yet fully stopped.

Three feet to the open doorway of the cab.

Two.

Rose threw herself inside.

A fire extinguisher hurtled past her, missing her face by inches. There was blood on the extinguisher. David lay sprawled beside the engineer's chair, a small pool of blood near his head.

Rose reached for the issue Beretta in the holster at her right hip. The holster flap was gone and so was the gun.

Makowski had David's Desert Eagle, the gun Rufus Burroughs had given him. He was trying to draw back the slide, stupidly not realizing that all he had to do was cock the hammer and pull the trigger.

Rose reached to her right side, tore at the buttons of the PSF camouflage BDU she wore, grasping the butt of the little Model 60.38 Special.

As Makowski fumbled with the Desert Eagle, the hammer cocked back.

There was a look in his eyes like something she expected in the face of hell's official greeter.

"Bitch!"

Rose fired as he pointed the gun at her face. There was a blur of motion, David's body lurching up, the Desert Eagle firing as a hole appeared above Makowski's left eye. Rose fired again, a second shot hitting him in the thorax.

Makowski's body crumpled back.

David lurched to his feet. He swayed there, leaning to the controls, then toward her. He reached for her, dropping to his knees beside her. "I hurt," she told him.

"He smashed all the controls, all of them. We've gotta jump. You first and—"

"No. Together. Remember?"

David touched his lips to her cheek. "Come on then, Rosie," and he hauled her up. She could barely stand.

David pushed her closer to the door.

They were into the shadow of the tunnel now.

"I even got your pistols out of the refrigerator," David told her, forcing a smile.

She could see them in his belt.

"As soon as we clear the tunnel."

The sound of gunfire was everywhere now, echoing and reechoing through the tunnel, from above, from all sides.

David aimed the Desert Eagle toward one of the drums of jellied gasoline.

"Jump fast and roll when I say it."

She said, "Yes, David."

The feeling in her abdomen sickened her. Something was happening to her she'd never experienced before. And inside herself, in the root of her soul, she knew what.

Tears streamed down her cheeks.

Light.

They were clear of the tunnel now.

David shouted, "Jump!"

Rose jumped as he fired the shot.

There was a flash of fire, and Rose Holden pitched through the air and into the snowbank, rolled, felt something snap under her, rolled, stopped.

A roar, louder than anything she'd ever heard in her life, and a wash of heat over her body.

The engine, exploding, she knew. She moved her good

right arm over her head, debris crashing down around her. Her BDUs were on fire. She tried to roll over into the snow. She screamed. Her right leg.

With her good right hand, she grabbed at snow, threw it onto the flames that spread along her left leg. She grabbed snow in handfuls, throwing it over herself.

The flames went out.

She tried to stand.

She screamed again with the pain.

Her right leg. She looked down along the length of her body.

Bone protruded through the leg of her BDU pants.

She dragged herself farther away from the track. "David! David!" The pain in her abdomen returned and so did the tears. "David!"

The baby.

"David!"

And she saw him.

He was moving, crawling through the snow toward her. The left side of his face was blackened. His left arm hung limp and twisted at his side.

"Rosie!"

Gunfire. Getting louder.

David rolled over onto his back.

There was a huge piece of metal sticking out of his left side.

"Jesus," Rose whispered.

She dragged herself toward him. His head turned toward her. "Get outta here, Rosie."

"Can't. Wouldn't if I could, David."

She dragged herself a few inches farther, touched her lips to his.

"Always," David said, blood trickling from the right corner of his mouth. He coughed and blood sprayed across his chest.

"They're coming." Rose saw PSF troopers with assault rifles running toward them from the roadbed. Behind them, the tunnel was still consumed with flame, what was left of the tunnel anyway.

She reached for the two pistols still stuffed in David's belt.

"Hold the butt for me, David."

David's right hand held the butt of the Detonics Servicemaster as Rose racked the slide back with her right hand.

"Now, keep that. It's my favorite gun, David. You know that?"

David coughed, nodded.

She caught the front sight of the Glock against the sole of her left boot, pushed the pistol forward and racked the slide.

Rose edged closer to David.

He sat himself up a little, coughing harder now.

PSF personnel closed toward them on both sides.

"I'm glad you're my wife," David said to her.

"I'm glad I am, too."

A spasm of pain went through her.

She locked her elbows against her sides, blinked.

David opened fire.

Rose opened fire.

PSF personnel fell to both sides of them.

Rose felt a bullet tearing through the right side of her chest, and she let the Glock fall from her fingers.

David sagged into the snow beside her.

The Detonics rolled out of his hand on the trigger guard, fell into the snow.

Rose Shepherd Holden felt David's hand as it touched hers.

CHAPTER THIRTY-THREE

Cameras and camcorders and microphones were everywhere around him as, with Borsoi and Montenegro and the escort of Presidential Strike Force personnel that had met them at the city limits, they entered the studios of the Metro network affiliate.

That afternoon, there had been talk of a Patriot attack on a military installation somewhere in the Northwest.

When they walked into the studio, he had heard more talk of it, casual conversation in hushed tones between the few real newsmen and the few real police there.

Borsoi had told him just before they'd left makeup, "Thad, this speech has just become more important than you could realize. The future of what we do here depends on you. I'll explain later."

"Gee. Don't worry, Mr. Johnson," Kearney told him in his best American accent. And together they walked along the narrow corridor to the Green room.

Montenegro waited there, a worried look knitting his brow. "It does not look good, Dimitri."

"What's wrong?" Kearney asked.

Borsoi shook his head. "It has nothing to do with you, except that your talk will be more important than ever, Thad."

Geoffrey Kearney lit a cigarette as he sat down to wait. And he thought of Linda Effingham.

In his mixed BDUs—black trousers, green blouse—and combat boots and pistol belt, he felt like somebody's war toy, which, indeed, he was.

There had been some question about their being armed as they'd entered the studio, but a word from the PSF officer in charge of their escort to the police official named Kaminsky settled that, Kaminsky in his peculiarly grating, high-pitched voice announcing broadly, "Let these men pass!"

Kearney never let the gun leave his side throughout the lighting and microphone level checks.

The pretty girl in the black dress who'd greeted them earlier on behalf of the producer entered the room. "We're on in five, gentlemen. Mr. Borden, may I show you the way?" And she gave Kearney a toothy smile.

Borsoi shook his hand. So did Montenegro. Borsoi said, "You'll do just fine, Thad."

"I have confidence that I will," Kearney said truthfully.

And he accompanied the girl with terminal cheerfulness.

They waited in the wings for several minutes while she told him again about red lights on cameras meaning the cameras were on and not to think about the cameras at all. "I know you'll do just great. You know, Mr. Borden, I kind of consider myself the average Jane. And gosh, what it says in the text of your speech makes a lot of sense to me. I'm sure the American people will love you."

Kearney smiled, but he could never do as good a job of that as she did. He thanked God for that.

After what seemed like forever, she told him, "Now, break a leg, like we say!" and she gave him a little shove.

He walked out onto the stage as the newsmen assembled to question him after the speech applauded politely.

Geoffrey Kearney ascended the platform.

He looked about him.

The red eyes of the television cameras glared back at him insolently. Good for them.

He pegged where Colin Best was seated. Just as rehearsed. Kearney judged the distance. Two paces. No—three.

He got the signal from the floor manager.

"People of America. A plague of violence has raged over the land. Who is responsible?"

Borsoi, seated just behind the newsmen, about ten feet away, nodded his approval. Montenegro, seated beside him, lit his pockmarked face with a fake smile.

"Is it the Front for the Liberation of North America? Is it the Patriots? I am the—" And he stopped. His next word was to be "Vindicator." Instead, Geoffrey Kearney let the American accent fall away as he stepped from behind the podium and walked toward the cameras, cutting the distance to Borsoi, Montenegro, and Best. "I am the man to tell you because I know both sides. The FLNA and President Roman Makowski work hand in hand for your undoing, the Patriots work for your freedom."

Kearney's gun was already drawn.

He'd checked the loads when he put the gun on his body to make certain he hadn't been slipped blanks because they didn't trust him. They trusted him. There was no accounting for bad judgment.

Geoffrey Kearney shot Dimitri Borsoi twice in the neck as Borsoi was pulling his pistol from the shoulder holster under his coat. Kearney wheeled right and shot Montenegro twice in the chest, then a third time between the eyes. He swung the muzzle of the pistol toward Borsoi again as he ran from the podium toward Colin Best. He fired, put out Borsoi's left eye. A Metro cop reached for him, and Kearney shoved him away, the muzzle of his pistol already to Colin Best's left temple.

"Shoot me and Colin Best is dead!"

As simple as that, Kearney thought. He'd gambled and, so far, was winning.

No one moved toward him.

From the darkness beyond the lights, the police official, Kaminsky, shouted to Kearney. Kearney remembered the simpering sound of the voice. Kaminsky wanted to know his demands.

So as Kearney drew Colin Best's sweating body closer to him and put the muzzle of the gun under Colin Best's right eye, Kearney announced, "There are FLNA personnel everywhere throughout this building inside and out. If I am attacked or interfered with in any way because I have shot these traitors to the American people, they will attack, and many, many of you will be killed. I want a fast police car with a police radio set to the correct frequency. I know the correct frequency, so no tricks. I want an aircraft waiting for me at Metro Airport, a 747, fueled and ready with an international pilot and charts for the Americas.

"Only once we are airborne will I announce my destination. Once I am landed safely, Colin Best will be freed."

And suddenly, the police and the Presidential Strike Force personnel started to do his bidding.

The commander of the PSF unit, a gruff captain named Carlsberg, said, "Ya'll was fuckin' with us all along, Limey."

Geoffrey Kearney pressed the gun tighter to Colin Best's face and told him, "Damn right."

Then Carlsberg shouted, "Get the son of a bitch whatever he wants and let him fly outta this shit town, heah?" And he looked at Geoffrey Kearney and laughed. . . .

Wisdom Twobears cleared his throat.

"And so, on this inauguration day, we remember those

who are still with us, who risked their lives—" He gestured toward the row just before him. "Sir Geoffrey Kearney, British ambassador, recipient of his own nation's Victoria Cross, a man who did what he did out of the pure love of what was right and pure hatred of what was wrong." Kearney nodded his head, his flowing white hair catching in the wind. He smiled.

"FBI Director-Designate Luther Steel, who along with the members of his almost legendary Metro Squad went so far beyond the call of any duty with which they could ever have been charged as to join that rare class of men and women known as heroes." Beside Steel, on his right, sat Steel's very pretty wife, their grown children in the row behind them. Seated with the adult Steel children was the oldest black man Wisdom Twobears had ever seen. He wore black, was rapier thin, and had a look about his eyes that was at once warm, yet hard as diamonds.

On Luther Steel's left, two chairs down, sat Tom LeFleur, between them white-haired and very old and frail, Clark Pietrowski. Two chairs were beside LeFleur, both empty, tied with black mourning ribbon, for Native American Special Agent Bill Runningdeer and Wisdom's friend of short duration and lasting memory, young Randy Blumenthal.

Beside them sat an old woman, the widow of one of the heroes, now gone. "The vacant chairs in this front row belong with perfect justice to Special Agents Runningdeer and Blumenthal; Special Agents LeFleur and Pietrowski are the only surviving members of Director-Designate Steel's Metro Squad. The woman beside them is the widow of Thomas Ashbrooke, killed several years after the Metro massacre and the attack on Fort Makowski.

"A smuggler, a modern-day privateer, Thomas Ashbrooke opened the flow of weapons to this nation, which, eventually, became substantial enough to allow the free people of the United States to turn the tide, win their freedom. He was killed in a storm at sea, when, at age seventy-four, he was bringing in a shipment of contraband medical supplies and ammunition in aid of the Charleston, South Carolina, Patriots, during high winds and seas. Three other ships with him got through and, as a result, an influenza epidemic within Charleston was thwarted and the Patriots were able to hold out against a renegade band of Presidential Strike Force personnel, eventually breaking their grip on the city and saving countless lives. Ashbrooke was a man who lived with a zest for life few modern men possess. Which is why he became the stuff of legend."

Wisdom Twobears extended his hands toward his mother and stepfather. "Matthew Smith, my stepfather, and Lilly Twobears Smith, my mother. Each in their own way heroes, Matthew Smith survived the attack on Fort Makowski, along with Director-Designate Luther Steel and my uncle, Bob Twobears." He gestured deeper into the audience, toward his uncle. "Matthew Smith and Luther Steel became the leaders of the Patriot Movement, guiding it into the alliance it became, which changed the face of a nation, perhaps the world."

Wisdom looked toward the statue. "Inscribed at the base of the statue we are about to unveil are names, although many were lost, many unsung. But to all, remembered and forgotten, the people of the United States and of the free world owe a debt that can never be repaid, only paid homage. These all have earned the ultimate title of respect: Patriots."

Wisdom Twobears nodded.

The coverings were drawn back from the statue set there at the center of the Mall.

Three figures dominated it.

Hands touching forever, battered bodies in the repose of

death, but their weapons in their hands as last gestures of defiance in the fight for freedom, were the lovers, Dr. David Holden and his wife of less than a day, Detective Rose (Rosie) Shepherd Holden.

Standing behind them, but ghostlike somehow, was the figure of a solitary man.

A black man.

There was a large handgun in his clenched right fist, and his left hand supported the staff of an American flag stiffened in a brisk wind.

His name was Rufus Burroughs.